FINDING DEATH

By

J.E. Taylor

Finding Death © 2024 J.E. Taylor
2nd Edition

All rights reserved under the International and Pan-American Copyright Conventions. No part of this book may be reproduced or transmitted in any form or by any means, electronic or mechanical, including photocopying, recording, or by any information storage and retrieval system, without permission in writing from the publisher.

This is a work of fiction. Names, places, characters and incidents are either the product of the author's imagination or are used fictitiously, and any resemblance to any actual persons, living or dead, organizations, events or locales is entirely coincidental.

For additional information contact:
www.JETaylor75.com

Warning: the unauthorized reproduction or distribution of this copyrighted work is illegal. Criminal copyright infringement, including infringement without monetary gain, is investigated by the FBI and is punishable by up to 5 years in prison and a fine of $250,000.

FINDING DEATH

When I set out to squash the reaper rebellion, I never thought having the positions of both Fate and Death would be a liability.

Boy, was I wrong.

Seriously, an ultimatum from Heaven never makes for a great start to the holidays. On top of the heavenly host trying to obliterate me, I've been cursed in the cruelest of ways.

I cannot touch anyone without destroying them.

If Heaven finds out about this particular affliction, I don't think even Sam and Dean would be able to stop the resulting Armageddon.

Chapter 1

I AM THE FIRST.

I'm the first offspring of Fate and Death that was conceived *after* they had taken the roles. In other words, they were not living, breathing beings when I was born. But the annihilation of the devil made so many weird things possible, including me.

I have no entry in the Book of Fates. Having no entry isn't normal. Every soul has an entry, a timeline that can be searched in the Book of Fates, but not me. In all of Earth's long and rich history, there has never been someone without an entry. To make matters more bizarre, I apparently can wipe out the entries of those I protect. So, now there are almost two dozen people running around like me with no written path.

The power to kill reapers has been solely Leviathan's gift. That, of course, does not include wielding either Heaven's blade or another ancient knife that was made just for that purpose. Those were the only things that could rid the world of a reaper. Until I unleashed my true potential. So, I am the first human to harness that little trick, and that was before I became a dual deity.

Which leads me to my current predicament. I now hold the role of both Fate and Death—while breathing, I might add, which is another historical event. Blood flows through my veins with every beat of my teenage heart.

I'm not the only one alive, either. It seems I've given my parents a moratorium on death, too. For the first time in decades, they have a steady heartbeat.

But all this mojo, all this ethereal juice, didn't come without a side effect, and what a doozy it is. I can't touch anyone. Well, except my father, but that's only because he touched me after my transformation into duel-deityship.

My touch isn't deadly per se. It's so much worse.

I absorb souls when my flesh connects with anything harboring a life-force.

So, although my dad is breathing again, he has no soul. Once his life is over, there will be no happily ever after for him and my mother in the land of the dead.

My only saving grace: Heaven does not know about my latest curse.

However, when they find out, I'm sure they'll send an army of assassins after me. Even now, just having a single being at the helm as both Death and Fate was enough to get Heaven's panties in a wad.

The trees pass as my father drives down the winding roads leading us home from Kittery. I glance at him for a moment as the silence surrounds us. His dark hair falls onto his forehead unchecked. The man doesn't look a day older than I am, and yet he had been Death for fifty some years. He gives me a smile and then looks back at the road, navigating us home. Well, to the only home that I've ever known, anyway.

My father seems pleased now that the first of my obstacles has been taken care of. Taking on the reapers wasn't all that challenging, in retrospect.

I guess having the power to annihilate reapers who harbor ill will toward me and my family helped, but it certainly made it anticlimactic. I mean, as soon as I wiped out half the reaper legion, the remaining horde of reapers bowed to show their alliance pretty damn quick.

Although stripping the reapers from existence didn't feel like my finest hour.

I huff at my internal dialog as my father pulls into the Ryans' driveway. The house is a pretty two-story colonial on a bluff overlooking the ocean. We can actually see Papa's house on Roaring Rock Road from our backyard.

"What?" my father asks from the driver's seat.

"She is just mourning those she killed," Levi, the German shepherd in the backseat, says.

He really isn't a dog but a monster in drag, protecting me from harm at the direction of my father. You see, Leviathan is seriously loyal to my dad because before my father even became Death, he set Leviathan free. I guess if I had been chained since the dawn of time and someone freed me, I'd be protecting them with everything I had, too. It's actually kind of sweet.

I look over the seat and roll my eyes at Levi. I'm not mourning the reapers I killed. Not really. Well, maybe. Damn, I hate he could read my deepest feelings.

The house looms before us, and I bite my lower lip. Before we left to deal with the reaper uprising, an emissary from Heaven had been sent to annihilate me. Thankfully, he has a mind of his own.

You see, Heaven sent Papa Ryan's dead brother back home to take care of the situation, but none of us truly knew what that meant. Luckily, Papa's brother didn't seem all that keen on carrying out their orders to destroy me. But that was before I took care of the reaper uprising.

Now that that particular roadblock has been taken care of, I don't know what will happen next.

"Are you coming?" My father had climbed out of the car while I was lost in my own mental review of my situation. He opens the back door for Levi.

The front door to the house stands open and the person in the doorway erases all the random thoughts piling up in my head.

Zane Bradley stands at the front of the growing group. His bright-green eyes lock with mine and the relief that washes over his features is enough to get me moving. He's really stunning to look at, with his dark hair gently shifting in the ocean breeze and his muscular physique that supports his side gig as a home improvement guy, but I would never in my wildest dreams tell him that. Just seeing him brings a smile to my face. I guess having my lifetime crush still present after the insane weekend we've all had is enough to light the fire underneath me.

My best friend, and de facto sister, elbows her way through to stand next to Zane. Her red hair blows in the breeze and if I could freeze this moment, I would. My victory seems small compared to the love that radiates from the house, and I slowly climb out of the car.

As I round the grill and step into the rays of the garage spots, Holly's mouth drops open. But it's Zane's slow smile as he scans me from head to toe that makes my heart skip a beat.

You see, I never changed from the leather outfit I conjured for my face-off with the reapers. And it is kick ass, with a fitted bodice and flared skirt with a slit that is probably too high for a sixteen-year-old. I guess I composed it right because it certainly has the effect on Zane that I had been going for when I put it together in my mind.

He licks his lips and starts toward me. But then his smile fades, and he draws to a stop. The glaring truth extinguishes his momentary excitement. He cannot so much as brush his hand against me, never mind wrap his arms around me and kiss me like I want him to.

My momentary spike of anticipation falls to the ground as effectively as a mic drop. It crushes my insides, turning my mood darker, and dropping me on the edge of despair. I almost turn and run because although I feel their love in waves, being near these people is dangerous.

At this precise moment, my father, who is the only one here who can touch me, throws his arm over my shoulder as if he knows I'm a flight risk and smiles at the crowd at the door. "She had them shaking in their hoods," he says with a grin, breaking through whatever darkness grabbed hold of me.

I roll my eyes and shake his arm off my shoulders. His explanation doesn't paint me in the light I want, although it's totally accurate. I had them quaking and dropping to their knees, but it wasn't out of respect. It had been out of fear. I was serious, too—if they ganged up on me en masse again, I would annihilate the lot of them, despite the ramifications.

Zane cocks his eyebrow and I know what the question floating in his mind is. I shrug. I had gone a little GoT on the reapers. The disappointment that flashes in his eyes and rounds his shoulders turns my stomach sour.

I'll have to fill him in later. I have one more dangerous enemy to deal with and its emissary steps out of the house. His dark hair blows in the breeze and his piercing blue eyes echo all those related to him by angle blood. I jut my chin out, staring him down like we were going to be thrown into a cage to fight to the Death.

His lips twitch into a cocky grin, as if he would welcome a bloody fight. But then he gives me a nod, like I have done something that he respects instead of something worthy of destroying me. Holly's Papa had once said he was the wild one of the two of them. The one who didn't always walk on the right side of the law, but he had lived through hell after their father died. Despite whatever trials Tom Ryan had been put through, Papa said he definitely had the bigger heart.

I certainly hope so, and that somehow I've won him over. Otherwise, I am walking into an ambush I am ill prepared to defend.

Chapter 2

IN THE FAMILY ROOM, I pull a kitchen chair into the corner, away from any chance of knocking anyone. I don't need another soulless person around who had no eternal future. The guilt over my father is enough to carry; I can't imagine that burden multiplied.

My mother remains in her spot in the kitchen, her gaze jumping between my father and me like she didn't know whether she wanted to hear what happened. She brushes a stray blonde hair out of her face and puts down the dishcloth she had been using when I walked in.

Zane drags a chair next to mine and sits as close as he dares without touching me. It's oddly comforting because I can feel his essence. It leaves me warm enough to sigh, even though everyone else is acting odd, as if I am a stranger.

Holly sits on the floor so the adults in the room can either congregate on the couches or at the dinner table that ends where the family room begins. She leans against the edge of the couch and crosses her arms. "So, are you going to clue us in as to what happened?"

I glance at the rest of the people in the house. Alex and Faith, Holly's parents, lean on the kitchen island with coffee cups. Alex runs his hand through his dark hair as he waits for me to answer, and Faith just keeps twirling a strand of her fiery hair on her finger. It is one of her nervous habits and I wonder what exactly was said while my father and I were dealing with the reapers.

Holly's Papa takes a seat at the kitchen table, along with his brother. I can tell who is related to the angels just by glancing around the room. Every single one of them has piercing blue, iridescent eyes. It reminds me almost of neon blue, especially in the low lights, like now. I've never seen eyes like that outside the family.

Usually, being the center of attention with Holly isn't a problem, but tonight it gets under my skin like a bad case of poison ivy. I refrain from itching my skin in response. Papa's brother's stare makes me shift in my seat. He is the one Heaven sent to destroy me, but he doesn't seem all that eager to follow Heaven's orders.

Although I'm leery of him, he isn't the one who sets off alarms in my head as my gaze passes over him. It's Kylee and her husband Michael who make me want to wield my scythe in self-defense. Every sense of mine tingles just looking at them, and Michael won't so much as look at me. Even Kylee averts her gaze when I glance her way.

Something is gravely wrong here, and it takes me a moment to realize what is missing. I scan the room and then tilt my head, listening for a television somewhere in the house. Nothing. No electronics of any kind are on.

"Where are your kids?" I address Kylee.

She barely meets my gaze. "We sent them over to CJ's house with Smoke and Phoebe to put them to bed."

Zane's nod confirms her statement. And it sounds reasonable, given it's late enough, but that didn't stop the warning bells in my head. Twisting, turning doubt blooms in my belly.

"Why wouldn't you go with your kids?"

"We, uh, we wanted to be here for you when you returned." Kylee stumbles on her words.

I nod and glance at the ground, rummaging around through Fate's memories swarming in my head. Alarms are sounding like the house is engulfed in flames, but I can't read Kylee. She is acting completely squirrelly.

"What happened?" Holly asks again.

I shrug. "Unfortunately, they wouldn't listen, and now there's a lot of dust and ash floating around Fort McClary."

She grins and her eyes sparkle as if this were one of her freaky supernatural shows instead of real life. She's enjoying this, but then again, Holly has always been twisted, so this is right on point for her character. She's warped, and for a minute, the binds of our friendship seem solid. But then she asks, "So, you toasted all of them?"

"No. I only eliminated those who would harm you." I let that sink in. I don't want the people closest to me to think I am some kind of bloodthirsty fiend. "Any of you." I glance around the room to make sure they know that extends to everyone here and not just my immediate family. "And any reaper who had a violent reaction to me taking both roles. The rest were willing to kneel to show their loyalty." At least, I hope they were going to be loyal.

Michael fiddles with something under the table and Kylee stares at him with a crease in the space between her eyes. They seem lost in their own thoughts, and those thoughts don't seem all that kosher.

I glance at Alex and then over to Michael, silently relaying my blooming concern with my eye movement. He's never been able to read me, but Alex and Faith and Papa can get into most of the people's heads in this room with their psychic connection. The silent communication between Alex, Faith, and Papa begins. Papa's eyes narrow and he cocks his head as though he picked up a bad wavelength.

"What are you doing?" he asks Michael, pulling everyone's attention away from me.

Even Papa's brother now looks at Michael with curiosity.

"Nothing," Michael says, but he continues to stare at the table, avoiding eye contact with anyone.

"Heaven sent you to kill me?" I ask, reading his face with a certainty that left me cold, but Papa's expression is downright chilling.

Michael hisses and reaches up to his temple, bringing his hands into view from underneath the table. One hand goes to his temple and the other stops with a glistening crystal-blue knife.

Whatever headache Papa is creating eliminated Michael's surprise attack, but he keeps his grip tight on the handle despite whatever pain he's experiencing.

Both Faith and Alex gasp at the blade he holds.

"You brought Heaven's blade?" The growl in Papa's voice slams home.

Faith's gaze jumps to my father. From what I gathered from all of Faith's stories of her run-in with Lucifer, she left Heaven's blade with Death.

But it clearly is now in Michael's possession. Anything even nicked with that blade ceases to exist.

My chest tightens. Heaven got to him, too. How many others in my close circle were doing Heaven's bidding?

My father's gaze narrows, as do his lips, and his eyes shift to Kylee. The former siren who procured ancient weapons as a hobby. She has almost every known weapon in the universe locked up tight in her fortress in San Diego. Except this one. Heaven's blade is here.

The last time Heaven's blade had been out in the general human population was when my mother faced off against an escaped demon. It was used to turn that rebel into dust.

14

And now, from the look on Michael's face, he means to turn *me* to dust.

One minute, Michael winces in pain, and the next, he launches the blade at me. I stare at it as it circles, end over end. If I dodge right, I plow into Zane and strip him of his soul. To my left is a wall. I'm stuck and as helpless as I've ever felt.

I'm not the only one shocked in the room, but someone recovers their wits because the blade stops less than a foot from my chest. He aimed it at the biggest part of me. The one surefire way to at least nick me if I wasn't fast enough to get out of the way.

Except Michael forgot one very important fact. He's in a room with the most powerful supernaturals on Earth. If he didn't forget, then he was betting on the shock factor.

The fact it came so close was a testament to his surprise attack. I don't know who saved my ass. It could have been Papa or Alex or Faith, because all three of them can control matter.

The knife hangs in the air for a moment and then drops straight down as if it were batted out of the air. It clangs on the floor and all eyes shift back to the one who had the audacity to try to kill me.

Michael pales and his gaze shoots to the ones with the actual power in the room. The ones who could crush him with just a thought. Alex actually growls and steps toward Michael. I thought he looked angry on career day, but my God, he looks like steam is coming out of his ears.

Papa puts his hand on Alex's chest, stopping him from giving Michael a physical beatdown with his fists.

Levi jumps from his position next to my father, and he lands on the table crouching, his nose elongating enough to show his true head, with teeth bared that are strong enough to bite through titanium steel.

"Levi," I say in a stern voice. He snaps back into regular form, looking at me in a cross manner. "No." I may be mad at Michael, but I don't want him dead. Beaten and bruised, maybe, but not killed. He was only following orders from Heaven, and I am not sure he understands the total ramifications if that knife nicks me.

Movement diverts my attention away from the table. Papa's brother crosses and picks up the knife, causing everyone to freeze. I hold my breath. He's close enough to wield that weapon, and there'd be nothing anyone could do if he tried. He's already dead and risen by Heaven's grace, so killing him wouldn't work.

"So, this is the famed blade that annihilated Lucifer." He studies it, careful not to touch the business end of the knife, and then he turns to

16

me. For a moment, I think he's going to finish what Michael had started, but then he hands the knife to me, hilt first.

I hesitate and meet Tom Ryan's humor-filled eyes. I reach out slowly, waiting for him to pull the knife back and brandish it, snuffing me out of existence. But he never flinches or looks away. I think it's his way of making peace with me. I now understand the kinship. I understand I'm more a Ryan in their eyes than I am a Ramsay.

I take the blade and do the same type of inspection that he had, wishing for the proper sheath to put this baby somewhere safe. A scabbard made of leather and steel appears at my waist. I stare at the conjured sheath and then carefully slide the knife into the case. It fits like it is made for the blade. This little trick of conjuring what I wish comes in handier than I thought.

Zane's eyes are locked on the blade at my waist, as if he is still trying to come to terms with this entire ordeal. I think Michael looks pale, but Zane looks a breath away from passing out. I want to reach out and squeeze his arm to reassure him, but I can't. Not with this godforsaken curse.

Touching him puts him in mortal danger. So, I ignore him for now and focus back on Michael. Anger fresh enough to make my hands shake accosts me, and I cross my arms. "Why?" I demand.

"You are an abomination. Borne of Lucifer's magic," he says, as if reciting what Heaven pounded in his head.

"Last I knew, Fate and Death were my parents, not Lucifer," I snap. I am done with this little show of morality. Especially from a vampire's son.

"How could you?" Faith snarls, her voice shaking. Faith's anger displays in sparks lighting from her fingertips. Hell, sparks are coming out of the ends of her hair, turning from the orange-yellow flame into a white light that I have never seen before. And I've seen Holly's mom angry before. This seems to be more like fury, almost to the point there is no reasoning with her at all.

"After coming into my home for so many years and breaking bread with us? How could you try to kill her?" Faith's voice even booms, rattling the dishes on the counters and the table. She clenches her fists as if she's afraid whatever manifestation inside her would be released into the entire room.

Nana puts her hand on Faith's shoulder, and although I can see the disappointment in Nana's eyes as she looks in Michael's direction, she has the desired calming effect Faith needs. The dishes stop rattling.

"It's a better alternative than true Armageddon. If the angels come..." Michael shakes his head. "We'll all die."

"You really think I'd let them harm you?" I shout, standing up to make my point very clear. "You really think I'm capable of that?" I want to reach across the table and shake him like a rag doll, and I take a step closer before I realize if I touch him, he'll be soulless. At least right now he looks a little remorseful; without a soul and with Heaven's directive, he'd stop at nothing to destroy me.

He leans back in the seat with wide eyes at my outburst. I usually take things pretty calmly with everything except where my parents are concerned, so me yelling is a big deal. The thing that sucks is no one can lay their hand on me to rein in my anger like Nana had with Faith.

A hand drops on my arm.

Well, my dad still can, but it did nothing to quench the burn in my veins. I stare at him.

"Cool your jets. I'll pound his fucking head in," he says with such malice that I think everyone blinks. I certainly do. He moves faster than anyone expects. Before I know it, he has a handful of Michael's shirt and his right fist smashes square into Michael's face.

Blood spurts from his nose and mouth, and Michael falls back in his seat, stunned.

"That is my daughter you just tried to kill."

"Dad, step away," I pull him back before he launches another punch. "An ultimatum from Heaven can't be easy to ignore."

Papa's brother scoffs. "Angels are dicks. I'll fight them with you." He gives me a cocky grin.

"You aren't equipped to fight against Heaven anymore." Faith steps closer to me. "But we are, so let them come." She glares at Michael. "So, you just run back to that goddamned portal and tell them they just screwed with the wrong family." She glances at Tom. "Or better yet, why don't you take me to Paradise Cove. I opened that portal. I can close it, too." She flips her hair over her right shoulder with an arrogance I had never seen in her.

Michael's eyes widen as he continued to cup his nose and mouth. Blood drips from his hands, enough for me to glance at my father. He has a mean punch for a mere mortal.

Papa glances at Faith with something akin to horror on his face. I know how much everyone in this room relies on the only portal to Heaven in the known universe to see their relatives. Even Faith goes from time to time to talk to her own mother, so the magnitude of her threat shakes everyone in the room to the core.

"What do you mean, everyone will die?" Zane asks from the chair where he still sat. He is

20

blinking fast, as if his brain can't digest the past few minutes. He looks at Michael and then at me as if he just awoke from a nightmare, only to find it's real.

"They told him he needed to take care of this now before the world went straight to Hell. This is an imbalance that can't be. Earth will collapse under the weight of it. Literally. So, if we don't do this, they will come down and do it and that will cause another big bang event."

"And what would have happened if you had cut me with Heaven's blade? What happens if there is no Fate or Death?" I ask, curious whether anyone knows the answer. My parents both pale. They held the knowledge crammed in my head. I cross my arms and wait. When no one answer, I add, "If Heaven kills me while I hold both positions, what happens?" I tap my foot, glancing at everyone in the room except for my parents.

"Everyone dies," Michael says slowly from behind his hands. His voice has a nasally quality as if he'd developed a terrible cold.

"Yup. And what happens if someone here kills me while I hold both positions?"

Michael starts to shrug and then his hands drop to the table, leaving bloody handprints on the wood. His eyes widen. Heaven's duplicity finally shines through. He understands, and from the faces surrounding me, everyone is already there; we just had to get both Michael and Kylee there, too.

"It makes no difference who kills me right now, does it?" I cock an eyebrow, spelling it out for him in simple words.

He slowly shakes his head as the reality of the situation sinks in. I am still a time bomb waiting to wipe out all of humanity. He glances at Papa's brother as if he would have some reasonable answer that would make sense.

"I told you. Angels are dicks." He shrugs. "They would be just as happy with or without humanity in the picture."

"They sanction mass murder?" Kylee gasps.

I slowly sit down. The reality of the situation claws at my insides. Heaven is not only ready to sacrifice me, but all of humanity.

Chapter 3

FAITH STILL LOOKS READY to kick some Heavenly ass, or at least close the only portal that gives angels access to this realm. Her fire hasn't faded since we all gave it a rest for the night. And today hasn't been any different.

We had been at this all day—arguing over who should do what—and the longer Heaven's portal is open, the more chances of being attacked come into play. Although with Alex and Papa setting their protective barriers around the houses, the angels had about as much of a prayer of entering as the demons of old.

The sun went down about an hour ago and my stomach rumbles. I am sick and tired of this conversation. I'm not one to sit around. I'm more of an action girl and all this inaction is driving me batty.

"Why don't you just give us the book and the scythe again?" my father asks after hours of discussing options. None of which are appetizing to anyone.

I glance at Levi and receive a cock of his eyebrow in response. Before I can second-guess myself, I hand my father the scythe, intending to let him take over again. Cringing, I wait for the transfer, but nothing happens. No swirl of wind, no ethereal light. Nothing. It's as if the scythe rejects him.

He looks down at himself and then back at me. "I don't feel any different."

"That's because nothing happened." I yank the scythe back before he can swing it around and hurt someone.

He glances at his empty hand and then at me as if I imparted some magic instead of ripping the ultimate instrument of death from his grip. He cocks his head. "Why didn't it work?"

I have one guess, but I keep my mouth shut. He is an empty vessel. Soulless. And I think the scythe knows it. The alternative is too weird to entertain, but it creeps into my head anyway. Perhaps the scythe, like the reapers, wants me in this position. Instead of answering him, I busy myself with shrinking the weapon into a charm again. I will not attempt to give my mother the Book of Fates and tempt the darkness weighing on me. Not when my gut tells me she will die, and I will be stuck forever with my mother telling me what to do. That is not a plan I can get behind at all.

Besides, knowing the person who takes over for either job will die makes this a categorical no for me to transfer the position to anyone else but my parents. And because the powers that be rejected my father, that was the end of the conversation.

"Seems like you're a little impotent there, kid." Smoke's New York accent is filled with mirth. He leans on the kitchen counter, picking at the leftovers. Smoke grins, enjoying my father's suffering just a little too much.

I would understand it more if he was yanking my mother's chain, considering Fate had kept him in cat form for millenniums. But that had been the entity before my mother. My mom actually found a loophole in Smoke's contract that allowed him to come back in this suave form. I wonder whether he can still shift into the

25

fearless form he had before Fate cursed him into a housecat.

"Fuck you." My father glares at him, but my mother's hand on his shoulder shut up whatever else was poised to slip out of his mouth.

Phoebe smacks Smoke on the arm. "Leave the boy alone." Phoebe and Smoke had come back with the kids during our earlier spirited debate, and neither of them had contributed much to the conversation at all until now.

"Give me the scythe." Zane holds his hand out.

If I could have batted it away without harming him, I would have. Instead, I just level the type of glare that had him pulling away without another word. Having him take over for Death isn't an option, especially considering that means he stops breathing.

"You idiot." Holly smacks his hand away as if she read my mind. "If anyone is going to step into this with her, it's going to be me," she says, and my gratefulness disappears.

Just as I'm ready to launch into a tirade, Alex does it for me.

"No way!" He yanks Holly back as if I am daft enough to hand her the scythe. "This isn't some fantasy game we are playing. This is Death. Death!"

26

"Yeah, and what better way to spend the rest of my life? With my best friend." She turns to me. "Think of the trouble we could get into!"

She grins in a way that makes me nervous and sad at the same time. I want her to go to college. To get married and have kids. I want to see her grow old with a husband who loves her more than I do. I cannot strike that down. Just like I can't let Zane do the same. Even though the relationship with him is much more complicated, it would still end messy.

"I'm not sure we would still be friends after a couple thousand years with only the two of us and Levi to keep us entertained."

Her shoulders drop and she seems to deflate before me.

"Look, while I appreciate the sentiments from both you and Zane, no one is taking over either role. If it had worked with my dad, I would have gladly given my mother the book of Fates. But it didn't, so I'll continue to hold these roles until all of Heaven is convinced I am not a menace."

"They'll keep sending more." Michael's voice is still nasally, and both eyes blackened like a raccoon from my father's earlier punch. He at least had gone into the bathroom to clean up before his kids arrived with Smoke and Phoebe. "But I doubt those they send next will be able to be reasoned with."

I roll my eyes. "Who are they going to send that these guys haven't already beaten?" I point to Papa, Papa's brother, Alex, and Faith. "They took on the devil and won. They hold the grace of all the archangels inside them, so who can they send? Who can beat them?"

Heat drains from my cheeks. There is only one being stronger than the collective power in this room. God himself. If they send the supreme being who made all of Heaven and Earth, we are screwed.

"God hasn't been around since they crucified his son," Levi says from the floor. "But that might be the only being that could snuff us all out."

My hand falls to the knife at my side and the thought that blooms in the back of my mind is unthinkable. I move my hand away and cross to the sliding glass doors. I am not about to voice my thoughts. Even having them at all is blasphemy.

"We need to close that portal," Faith says, but at least this time it is with a more reasoned tone. "That will stop them from sending more..." She waves toward Michael. "More gullible idiots."

"I agree with Faith," my mother says, and I turn toward her. She hasn't said much through all of this. Not since my father agreed to take the roles back, and the transfer didn't happen. "We

28

can at least mitigate the number of people gunning for her."

"If we close the portal, does that prevent them from launching this war?" Papa asks. The worry lines around his mouth and on his forehead express his unease.

I totally understand his hesitation. That portal is the only place the family can see their loved ones who have passed on. If that was the only way I could see my parents, I'd be hesitant, too. I don't think he is prepared to say final goodbyes to all who he has lost in his life. He glances at his brother.

Tom shrugs.

"They'd have to go through Purgatory." My father glances at Levi. "And no one is guarding the gates there anymore. After she wiped out half the federation in Kittery, I doubt the reapers would put up much of a fuss if the angels went through that way, either."

That was my fault. I close my eyes and lean my forehead against the cool glass, berating myself silently. I didn't exactly instill loyalty with the reapers last night. Fear, yes, but true alliances? Not a chance—and that's really what I need. "Can we do this in the morning? I'm not up for a midnight drive across New Hampshire."

"You aren't going," Alex says.

My eyebrows rise in the reflection, and I turn away from the glass door. "If closing that portal puts Faith in danger, you bet your ass I'll be there."

He scoffs at me. "You aren't equipped to handle that kind of attack. We are."

"I can toast reapers. You don't think I can conjure up some powers to take on angels?"

My father snorts a laugh.

I give him the side eye, but that doesn't stop his continuing chuckle. Although his laughing at me is aggravating, he is right. I am not sure my personal karate training from Alex and Papa was enough, especially because I haven't trained in a while. I know my way around a multiple attack scenario, but even if I wanted to get a few sparring sessions in before we leave, I can't train hand-to-hand.

"If you are going on this crazy mission, so am I." I cross my arms. "I'm not letting anyone get hurt because I acted on impulse." Taking the scythe from my father had been on impulse, especially considering I somehow made it so my mother was living. I hadn't wanted them separated. That bleeding-heart part of me is exactly what made me grab it from his hand and caused this lousy touch side effect.

"You can't step on that hallowed ground," my father says after he winds down. "You are Death.

30

You can never cross over into Heaven's territory. Just like you will never cross into Hell's territory either. Your domain is the between."

I blow a raspberry at him. "Everything about me challenges the status quo. You really believe I can't step into their domain? Especially when they've decided to invade mine?"

He wipes his face and looks at my mother for help.

"Honestly, she has a point," my mother says.

"Well, if you're going, so am I," Zane says.

"No," everyone in the room says at the same time, including me. I don't want him anywhere near the angels. That's like handing them the ultimate leverage.

Zane leans back in the chair and scans every face in the room before his gaze lands on me. And damn, he's got a stubborn jaw. "I'm going."

"For Christ's sake!" Faith throws her hands in the air and walks out of the room.

No one moves. Then a car engine starts up.

"Damn it," Alex snarls and stalks out after her.

"I guess we are all going to the lake house," Papa says with a shake of his head. He glances at the food strewn about the kitchen and closes his eyes. A small vein on his forehead bulges, and then a drawer opens and the press-and-seal wrap comes out as if carried by the invisible man. Each item is wrapped with speed and precision, and then everything floats in the air toward an open refrigerator. When everything is placed on the shelves, the door closes.

Papa doesn't even break a sweat at the effort. Sometimes I wish for that kind of juice. But my own powers aren't anything to scoff at. Although I would not want to be pitted against Papa.

"That just about does it." He glances at Michael and Kylee. "If you two want to stay here and put your kids down, I'm sure Alex and Faith won't mind."

"I think I'd like to say one last goodbye to my folks before Faith wipes out the portal," Michael says.

I glance at Papa's brother. "Are you going with us?"

He nods slowly. "My wife and daughter are up there, and as much as I'd like to join your war against the angels, I don't wish to be separated from them for what is likely to be the rest of eternity." He glances at Papa. "I kind of screwed the pooch on this one, so I'm not sure they'll allow me back, but I have to try."

"And if I could pull them out?" I ask. After all, I pulled my mother and father's life-force from wherever it had gone, reanimating them after fifty some years of not being alive.

"You can't," my mother says, as if my suggestion is too terrible to even consider. As if it is more horrifying than Heaven's intentions of taking me out and all the fallout that will come from that debacle.

"Why can't I?" I cross my arms. "What if I could bring them all back?" I wonder whether I really have that sort of power. It would be interesting to find out. I even had the list of names in the back of my mind.

"Because it would cause a major imbalance in the universe."

"So? There already is an imbalance, according to Heaven."

"It's not the way to win brownie points with them. Stealing souls from their care is frowned upon. Just like screwing with Fates."

At this moment, I don't give a damn about winning them over. Heaven burned that bridge when they sent Michael and Kylee to kill me. Closing the portal will hurt those I care about. I can see it in their eyes. If Heaven can reanimate Papa's brother, why can't I do the same with the people my family cares about?

"We can talk on the way." My father grabs one of the key sets on the wall next to the garage entrance. "Missy gets the passenger seat. Zane, Levi, and Julia, you get the back. The rest of you need to move your cars out of the way. I'm taking whatever these keys go to." He jangles a set of keys.

"I'm going with you." Holly follows as my mother starts toward the door with Levi. Zane joins our mini entourage.

I weave through the remaining guests until I am clear of the family room congestion. "We'll see you up there." I don't wait for anyone's response. Closing the door, I press the garage opener and by the time I climb around to the passenger side, the door was up, and the cool night wraps an unspeakable dread around my heart.

Chapter 4

"DO YOU EVEN KNOW where you're going?" Holly asks from the backseat.

We arrived in Brooksfield, New Hampshire twenty minutes ago and all my father has done is drive in circles, muttering under his breath. He sends a glare into the rearview mirror.

"Do you?" he barks at Holly.

"Yes." Holly doesn't bother explaining where we need to go. She just crosses her arms and cocks her head at my father.

"You want to drive?" he snaps and pulls the car to the side of the road. Without another word, he throws the shift into park and steps out of the car. He opens the door behind him and waits for Holly to get out.

She looks at him with wide eyes.

"You're old enough to drive, so get us where we need to go before your mother fucks everything up."

Wow, dude, chill. I don't think I've ever seen my father this annoyed.

Holly climbs out of the backseat. "Are you sure?"

He sighs and stares her down in a way that would move my butt just as fast.

"Fine." She slips into the driver's seat and before my father can close the backseat door, she shifts into drive. With no one on the road in front of us, she does a U-turn, turning back the way we came.

"Do you know where we are going?" I never paid attention to the roads and turnoffs to get to the lake house. My nose was either in a book or taking in the scenery, so when she nods and takes a left turn into an overgrown driveway, I am impressed.

She glances at me as she slows to a crawl, maneuvering the road like an old woman. But in her defense, the driveway is narrow, and she is an inexperienced driver.

I want her to go faster. I want to get there because my nerves are dancing like I'm sitting on a bomb made of liquid nitrogen and dry ice. The explosion is imminent. When we round the corner, Holly slams on the brakes. The driveway is already full. Our wandering aimlessly left us last to arrive instead of right after Faith and Alex got there.

I don't wait for her to throw the car in park. I am out of the passenger side of the car, running toward the light show strobing through the trees. I stop halfway across the lawn as a body is thrown clear of the woods by what I assume is some righteous agent of Heaven in Paradise Cove.

The motion sensors on the house trigger and the back lawn lights up like it's midday. It takes my eyes a moment to adjust. Tom Ryan slowly sits up, his face forming a mask of anger and disgust. The names of the dead related to our family flit through my mind. I don't have much time. I kneel and place my hands on the ground. I believe I am close enough to the gate to affect the dead, so I call the souls forth.

I am not sure where to start until my eyes land back on Tom. I need to start with the one who defied Heaven's orders, because he is right—Heaven will never let him back in. I recite their first names aloud, including his. Wishing life into forms that come forth in my mind's eye.

"Tom, Ty, Jessica, Steve, Jennifer, Raven, Hannah, Damian, Naomi, Gabriel."

Light brighter than the spots settles over Tom, sparkling the way Nana's healing magic does when she uses it, making me pause before I complete the list in my mind.

I doubt Tom notices. Not when his mother and father step out of the woods. His father, Alex's namesake, is a spitting image of Alex, with those piercing blue eyes and dark hair and the kind of looks that make most women swoon. But he wasn't a saint when he was alive. From what I understand, Ty Ryan was quite the opposite, enough so that I don't know how he ended up in Heaven. Maybe it had to do with having angel blood. Tom's mother, Jessica Ryan, is pretty in a way that is just as striking as Ty Ryan. But it is her eyes that draw me in. Calico eyes like Nana's, but in tones that seemed to settle into a soft brush of color surrounded by that angel-blood blue.

Next comes Tom's guardians: Steve and Jennifer Williams, the original owners of the land I stand on. Although they really never understood their property housed the only portal

38

to Heaven. He had been an FBI agent before he and his actress wife settled in New York City. Both of them look as lost as Alex's grandparents.

Tom's jaw drops open and his eyes bulge when the red-haired mother and daughter step from the woods. Raven and Hannah, Tom's wife and daughter, don't seem as bewildered as everyone else, and their faces split into broad grins at the sight of Tom sitting on the lawn.

I hear a gasp from behind me and glance over my shoulder as Michael rounds the corner, with Kylee following close behind. Michael's parents and brother had already stepped onto the grass at the edge of the woods.

One by one, they glance around as if they had just woken from a long, drawn-out nightmare.

"Stop," my father orders from behind me. "You can't raise the dead," he hisses, and I glare back at him.

"That is precisely what I'm doing." There are more souls I want to call from Heaven, but before I can utter Faith's mother's name or my grandparents' names, a blinding white light fills the woods, making shadows run.

Screaming filters out of the woods, and curses that would make a pissed-off sailor proud carry on the wind. Papa stumbles out of the forest, followed by Alex, who is dragging a ballistically furious Faith with him. She never curses, but the foul words still spitting from her lips make everyone stare at her with open-mouth shock.

I wonder just what transpired in the portal. What words could Heaven have delivered to set the normally calm woman into this holy terror, complete with sparks shooting from her fingertips?

Papa draws short at the sight of the growing crowd and Alex bumps into him. It's almost like watching a comedy show, except everyone is too shocked to laugh. Silence descends on the clearing as the view of the crowd quiets Faith. Papa blinks as if his brain can't comprehend what he is seeing and then he turns toward where I still crouch.

I'm pleased by the arch of his eyebrow and the hint of a smile that captures his lips, like he can't quite believe what I've done. I shrug and offer a smile of sorts in his direction. Heaven may have initially given Papa his brother back, but I made it permanent, like I had with my parents. I yanked these souls from Heaven's grip and willed their bodies back into existence. None of which took any effort. I didn't even break a sweat.

They are here, living and breathing and just as fragile as the rest of us, but they don't have whatever powers they had when they were here. They had already passed those on and there was no time to recreate that. They are no longer gods among men. That is reserved for Papa, Nana, Alex, Faith, and Holly only. And from the awe widening Papa's eyes, apparently, I fall into that category, too.

No one moves at first, and then pandemonium breaks out in the form of hugs and even tears as they realize they've been given some strange gift. A chance to pick up where they had left off.

"What have you done?" My mother gasps. She goes to grab me, but my father intercepts her hand.

He shakes his head, his eyes warning her against touching me. "There's no sense in you losing your soul, too," he says to her.

I climb to my feet, satisfied with what I have accomplished. "If Heaven is going to send assassins to kill me, I need an army of loyal people to stand with me. And we both know the reapers will not fight at my side." I meet my father's gaze.

"You could have persuaded them," he says. "Instead, you brought these people back, only to face Death at the hands of the angels?"

I blink as his words scrape over my skin like an unwanted rash. I glance out at the people hugging and crying and expressing such joy that it fills my heart with dread. I signed every one of them up for doom unless I can figure out how to take on the angels without anyone being harmed. Maybe I need the reapers after all.

"How do I persuade them?" I ask as the crowd moves in our direction.

"I don't know. But this will have huge ramifications. You're supposed to reap the souls and escort them to their final destination, not revive them." He runs his hands through his hair and glances at my mother. For someone without a soul, he looks more worried than his current state allows.

I don't want to address his comments, not with everyone coming toward me like I am their savior. Tom puts his hand on his chest and his eyes widen. He stops short and a couple of the resurrectees bump into him.

"My heart," he says with his eyes glued to me. "What kind of necromancy shit is this?"

"It's not black magic," Raven, his wife, takes hold of his arm. "It's pure." She sniffs the air as though there is something sweet and decadent cooking.

He glances at her as if she has two heads.

"Can't you taste it? It's like a bowl of strawberries and whipped cream. Sweet and wholesome. Dark magic does not taste like this."

I stare at the redhead next to Tom and a plethora of information bubbles to the surface. She knows her way around practical magic, the kind I might need to lift this damn touch curse. But we have bigger worries, like what ramifications this little event will cause. I do not know, but my father is right. There will be hell to pay for my actions.

Papa's father, the feared Ty Ryan, steps forward and sticks his hand out toward me like he expects a handshake.

I jump back, colliding with my father.

"Don't touch her unless you want to become soulless like me," my dad says from behind me. "While she can make you come back to life, she can also ruin any chances of anything more than the here and now with her touch."

"Thanks, Dad," I mutter under my breath. I press my hands together and give a slight bow in salutation instead of accepting his handshake. "My father is right. He's the only one who can touch me at the moment, and I certainly hope that doesn't change."

"Who are you?" Ty asks. His question is framed in reverence.

"She's my daughter," my father says, pride oozing over every word.

Papa's father looks him over, his eyes narrowing. "And you are?"

I forget, most of these people never knew Death and Fate existed before they passed and went to Heaven. Tom knew because he had personal experience with my parents when the Ryans met Kylee, but the rest of them had already died by that point.

"I used to be Death and my wife here used to be Fate. But now our daughter has taken on both those roles and given us the ability to breathe again after fifty-four years." He shrugs like this all makes perfect sense and this is just another normal day.

Eyes move back to me.

"And Heaven is pissed at her." Faith speaks for the first time since Alex carried her out of the woods. Her voice is hoarse and bitter. "They want her dead, except killing her wipes out the world, and Heaven does not give a shit if this world dies." Faith spits on the ground as if she had just tasted something vile. "So, I closed their damn portal to Earth."

"You what?" Papa's father glances at his wife and then back at Faith.

"I used angel fire to destroy the only portal Heaven has." She points toward the cove. "It will take them forever to drill through to this realm." She crosses her arms as if she has just

44

conquered Heaven herself. "And I'm fine with that."

"Mmm." My father cocks his head. "You forgot one little hiccup."

Faith glances at him and cocks her head.

"Purgatory and the reaper realm."

Her stubborn expression falls, turning the edges of her lips down.

None of the reapers will put up a fight to stop my demise. I need to figure out a way to get them on my side before Heaven compromises that entry to Earth.

With this crew and the reapers on our side, we'd be unstoppable.

46

Chapter 5

THE LAKE HOUSE IS a tad tighter than Alex's house. We really should have gone back to Papa's place in York, where there is plenty of room for the crowd. Every time I move, I'm afraid I might brush someone by mistake and eviscerate their soul. It is far from a pleasant feeling.

I've shoved myself in the farthest corner and my father took it upon himself to take one side and Zane sits on the other side of me. At least Zane is far enough away that if he talks with his hands, he will not brush into me. I can't say the same for my father. It's as if he doesn't recognize personal space at all.

I'm antsy to get back to Maine, to where I know my surroundings and have ample room to work with. If we had stayed outside, I don't think the anxiety pulsing through me would have been quite as bad as it is right now.

One thing is for sure, these people can talk a subject to Death. We've all introduced ourselves, but I think the newly living are still having a hard time connecting all the dots.

"So, you are Lucifer's daughter?" Damian asks in a tone filled with disdain as he stares at Faith. He grips the arms of the chair so hard his knuckles turn white. It's the same type of reaction that Faith said Tom had at one time before he got to know her. He obviously changed his mind about her because he died so she could live.

Naomi, Damian's wife, reaches out and covers his hand. "She is the one who used Heaven's blade on him."

"While he possessed my daughter," Damian nearly growls.

Faith made me possible when she killed Lucifer. Her actions seventeen years ago changed the course of many lives. And saved the world from Armageddon. Unfortunately, we are back at another Earth-ending point. You'd think the Ryans would have this planet-saving down by now, but they are stumbling through it right alongside me.

"Yes," Faith answers, and there isn't an ounce of apology in her tone. The tension in the room thickens.

"Dad," Gabriel interrupts, trying to be the one to smooth over the friction before it blows up on all of us. "Faith did the right thing then, and she did the right thing now by closing that portal." He looks at his brother, Michael. "I still can't believe they'd sacrifice the world because some sweet teenager holds the role of both Death and Fate. And they didn't tell you this before they sent you to kill her?"

The fact he refers to me as sweet is humbling. I'm not sweet. I just did what I thought was necessary to win this war, and I didn't want Tom separated from his family after he defied Heaven's orders for a complete stranger.

Michael slowly shakes his head.

"So, let me get this straight. Heaven is just as fucked up as Hell?" Smoke asks. He's leaning against the wall, with Phoebe lounging against his chest. He glances at my mother as if she should know all this.

"I wouldn't know. I just had the reapers escort people to their assigned destination." She picks at her thumbnail. "I went by what the book told me."

I glance at the miniature book hanging from my charm bracelet and then back at her. Fates of men are already predestined, but their final destination isn't scripted. It's based on how they live their lives, but now I wonder by whose measure it is based.

"We got the files on those coming through Hell. They all deserved to be on my table." Phoebe crosses her arms.

Damian swings his darkening gaze to her. "Who are you?"

I've had enough of the posturing and climb to my feet. "Everyone in this room is family. So please leave the attitude outside." I glance around the room at the angel descendants I called from Heaven. Bright-blue eyes stare back at me. Every single pair holds almost an iridescent glow. They all carry an aura I can almost see, unlike those not born of angel blood. Steve, Jennifer, and Raven don't have those features, although Steve's eyes are an enviable blue. Smoke and Phoebe don't carry that same angel quality, either.

My father has the blue eyes that rival the angel kin. But he was born into an ethereal bloodline himself. My eyes weren't. My original color falls into the golden category, but now they seemed to have changed to a weird lavender. I really envy the neon blue of those with ethereal blood.

Papa's father chuckles. "Damian's not used to having others as old as he is in the room." He gives a head nod to Phoebe and Smoke.

"Aww, he's just a young'un." Smoke smiles. His New York accent drawls through the words like a car wreck.

"Actually, we are older than he is," Kylee says from next to Michael.

Damian turns and stares at her before his gaze moves to his son.

Michael shrugs. "She kind of fell right into my lap." He grins and drapes his arm around Kylee's shoulders. "But you knew that already."

"All this is well and good, but we really need to figure out what Heaven's next move is. Otherwise, we are going to be blindsided. And that never turns out well." Alex stands from the dinner table. He turns his back on all of us and stares out the window.

"We need the reapers," Levi says from his position on the floor.

Everyone who I called from Heaven turns ashen when the German shepherd speaks.

"Since when are there talking dogs?" Steve says.

Levi chuckles. So do Alex, Faith, Kylee, my mother, and my father. I crack a smile and meet Zane's gaze.

"Well, sir." Zane speaks first. "He's not really a dog."

"Yeah, he really wouldn't fit in the house if he was in his natural state," Faith says.

"What is he?"

"Leviathan," my mother says. "The guardian of the gates."

"Like, as in the fabled Leviathan?" Steve says, his eyebrows arched.

"Yes," Levi says. "And I'm bound to protect Missy," he adds. "So, anyone in this room thinking about harming her," he looks pointedly at Michael, "I will eat you." As if to make his point crystal-clear, he lets his head transform into his natural form, and then he snaps his sharp teeth with a ferocious growl before shrinking back into a dog.

Steve shifts back in the chair with wide eyes. "And I thought vampires were a stretch," he mumbles loud enough to make most of us smile.

"There are far more things out there than you silly humans can truly comprehend," Levi says with an eye roll.

Smoke snorts and glances out the window. A crease between his eyes appears, and I follow his gaze.

Alex steps backward as a sea of black accented by the spotlight stands out against the green grass. It looks like the entire reaper federation has shown up on the lawn, unbidden. I get to my feet and, without a word, head outside to deal with this mess. Before the door closes behind me, Levi shoots out and trots next to me like a sentry Hell-bent on protecting his charge.

By the time we round the corner, Levi has stripped himself of his dog persona and towers over all of us. It is a less than subtle warning. With one sweep of his tail, he could destroy the reapers and the house behind us. I ignore the gasps from inside as we step into view. I imagine those newly living are reeling at seeing the full effect of my trusty sidekick, or at least what they can see of him considering he towers over the trees. It's like looking out and seeing the hindquarters of a dinosaur in the window.

I keep my hands free, although I itch for my scythe. Pulling that into my hands would be seen as a sign of aggression, and I do not want to project that the way Leviathan is. I stop and turn, facing the skeletons as they look up at me with what I assume is malice. But without bodies, I can't tell, and I rely on body language to give me proper warning. I press my lips together, wishing they all had their original forms so I could truly tell their intentions.

Light fans out from me, touching every reaper. The scene reminds me of the lightning that shoots out from the ark in that old Indiana Jones movie. Except the reapers don't turn to dust at the touch of my light.

Instead, they grow human forms under their black capes. I step back, just as surprised as the reaper federation in front of me, as the light dims and faces of all shapes and colors stare up at me. Some with awe, some with confusion. Some just stare at their flesh-colored hands as though I have given them an unspeakable gift.

My father steps out from around the corner and halts as he scans the crowd.

"What is she?" one reaper in the front row asks, glancing at my father.

My dad is at a loss for words. He just stares at the reapers with human skin, his eyes blinking rapidly and his mouth forming a little O of shock. When he turns to me, he asks, "Did you just bring them all back to life?"

I don't know. All I wanted was to see their faces, and here they are. I shrug. "I don't think they are alive." I turn to the dark-haired woman who asked what I am. "Are you?"

With wide eyes, she puts her hand on her chest.

My heartbeat thunders in my ears as I wait for her to answer. If I truly breathed life into them, I was screwed. There would be no one to escort the dead.

She moves her hand again. And again, and then shakes her head. "No heartbeat." She glances at the reaper next to her and puts her palm on his chest. "None there, either."

The tension between my shoulders relaxes. I hadn't screwed up after all. "What's your name?"

"Amanda," she says. "But my friends call me Mandy." She sticks out her hand for a handshake.

I'm regretting our customs. Why couldn't I have been born in a place that bows as a salutation instead of shaking hands? I stare at her offered hand, wondering whether it's an invitation to call her Mandy or not.

"I am not trying to be rude, but this"—I wave at my form—"came with a nasty side effect and I'd rather not do any harm to your soul." I know better than most that reapers are souls who had agreed to forgo their final destination to serve Fate.

Mandy lowers her hand slowly. She swallows and glances over her shoulder. "Heaven sent us." She looks back at me and then down at her human hands.

Levi growls, and I put my hand out to calm him. I don't need to touch him to silence him; my motion is enough to quell any thought of an attack.

"If you try to harm her, I will destroy every single one of you," Levi growls.

"I think they get that." I look up at him as a few nervous laughs break out in the crowd. I glance back at the sea of faces and although I don't see any malice visible, I have to ask. "What are your intentions?" I aim my question at Mandy while suppressing the urge to send out my sweeping guide to snuff out the infiltrators.

"Heaven wants you destroyed." Mandy shifts as she studies her flesh-covered bones as if she has never seen skin before.

"And you came to do that?"

She continues to stare at her hands. Her mouth opens and closes a few times before she looks up at me with pleading eyes.

"You realize killing her takes out the entire world, right?" my father snaps.

Eyes widen and Mandy's gaze shoots from her hands to my face. She blinks as my father's words sink in.

Murmurs build to a crescendo all around us.

I laugh under my breath. Heaven seems to have left that little nugget out of the equation. And it matters to the reapers. It matters a great deal. When the world ends, they automatically move onto their final destination. Although some are headed for the pearly gates, especially those who were relatives of Death's, many chose to be reapers because the alternative was not Heaven.

Reapers, as a whole, aren't saints.

"I don't know if any of you were around when Death and Fate were created, but they were one entity like Missy here, and I guess Heaven wasn't too happy about that then, either. When Heaven destroyed that entity, this universe was created. I am not too keen on doing that to the Earth. Are you?"

Mandy opens her mouth and closes it and then stares down at the ground. "Heaven said you stole some souls from them." She looks beyond me at the picture window of the house, where everyone is watching.

"I figured if the person who raised me was going to close the only portal to Heaven, I'd pull out those they visited with the most. Unfortunately, I didn't get everyone out before she destroyed the portal with angel fire." I nod. "So yes. I did technically steal souls from Heaven and breathed life back into them."

"You raised the dead?" Her voice cracks. "That isn't supposed to be one of your powers."

Now I do laugh. "Neither is turning reapers to dust. But I seem to have had that power even before I became this god-awful entity."

"How?"

The answer to that question seems so much more complex. I don't understand how it truly works. All I know is when I wish for something to be, it happens. I wished them alive, and they lived. I wished reapers to have forms so I could see their expressions and here they are. On Thanksgiving, I wished for my family to be safe from harm, and they were. Even at the fort in Kittery, I wished the reapers with bad intentions gone. Maybe it isn't as complex as I thought, but it certainly is a dangerous gift. "I willed it," I finally say.

A new thought dawns. Could I will my touch not to be lethal to the soul?

I blink the thought away and refocus back on Mandy. "I haven't exercised the same magic that I did back at the fort to ferret out those who wish me ill will. But I can if I need to." Some reapers shift from foot to foot. I switch my gaze back to Mandy. "I'm assuming you are the one speaking for the rest?" I raise an eyebrow.

She nods slowly.

"What are your intentions?" I cross my arms. I am still uneasy about their alliances.

She takes a deep breath. "Well," she starts and looks at her hands. Her thumb strokes the side of her palm. "Before we knew the ramifications, we were going to follow Heaven's orders." She looks up at me. "Or at least die trying. Then you did this." She raises her hands, turning them palm forward and then palm back and lets out a huffing laugh. "And you brought back the dead." She points to the house. "So, honestly, I don't quite know what to do now."

At least she is honest.

"Do we get to keep this form?" a male reaper from a few rows back calls out.

"I can turn you all back if you'd prefer," I say, unsure whether he is happy about the change or prefers the skeleton form that they've had for millenniums.

"Oh, no. Please don't!"

Almost every reaper seems to agree, but I catch a couple of unsure expressions. If there is even one dissenting voice in the group, I can't expect them to be united with me against Heaven.

"Whoever would like their skeleton form back, raise their hand." I wait.

After a moment, two hands slowly rise in the air. That's it. Only two in a sea of hundreds. The rest of the reapers wrap their arms around their new substantial forms, as if to safeguard it from whatever may be coming.

"It's okay. Come forward, please." I wave the two hands toward me.

They step to the front of the crowd. They aren't the most stunning creatures in the pack, but they had their own beauty hidden within the thinning blonde hair and ruddy complexions. They look as if they feel like squat makeup artists in a room full of supermodels. The two are noticeably similar, as if they were siblings in the real world before they passed on. They shine in their own unique way.

"You really want to be a skeleton?" I ask, unsure whether that is their true want, or whether they are just embarrassed at their former bodies in comparison with the others. "Because you two are beautiful." I don't want them to regret the decision, and I certainly know all too well what it is like to feel different and gawky, even though others tell me I'm beautiful.

They look at each other and then around them. "We aren't..." They glance back at me.

"I only ask because I don't want you to regret your decision." Honestly, I don't know whether I can just zap only two of them back into skeleton form or whether it would affect the entire federation, but I don't want to say that out loud. This wishing or willing or whatever thing I'm doing is not an exact science, and I do not want to jeopardize what I think I've accomplished with the rest of the reapers.

They entwine their hands together and take a deep breath, searching each other's gray eyes.

I wait and scan the rest of the reapers, silently praying they will accept themselves as they are right now, because if I try to turn them back, and turn the rest of the group with the effort, I will lose my edge.

After what seems like eons, they turn back to me. "We will stay in human form for now," the shorter of the two says, satisfied with whatever silent communication they had between them.

The relief almost makes my shoulders sag, but I don't want to show any weaknesses right now. Something deep down forces me to remain strong when I really want to drop into a de-stressed puddle.

"So, now what?" Mandy asks, pulling my gaze to her as the other two fade back into the crowd.

61

"Now you bring me back to Purgatory so I can make sure no punks from Heaven break through the barrier to this realm," Levi says from next to me. He shrinks down into his dog form and steps closer to Mandy.

I'm not ready to lose my trusty sidekick. Without him, I'm not sure I'm the pillar of strength that I project when he's got my back.

Levi glances at me and gives me an eye roll, like he thinks my thoughts are juvenile. I suppose they are, but still, he makes me feel invincible.

"There's a war coming. Are you sure you want to be on the front line?" I ask him. I know it's a stupid question. This is Leviathan, after all. He glorifies war and eating whatever suits his fancy, whether it be demon, or reaper—or, in this case, angel. He cocks an eyebrow at me in an echo of my own thoughts. I glance around at the reaper federation surrounding us. "I don't want them on the front lines, either. Much less you." I meet Levi's gaze.

"This is what I was created to do," he says. "Heaven. Hell. Neither one is supposed to be able to punch through the fabric safeguarding Earth. It is the reapers' job to protect the reaper realm from attack as much as it is to escort souls to their final destination. It is mine to make sure nothing gets out of either Heaven or Hell through Purgatory."

Damn, he was one loyal creature. And I know that's what he is designed for, but it doesn't make the lump forming in my throat any smaller. I swallow it anyway.

I can't let the reapers see me cry. I blink back the swell of tears and glance at Mandy. "I'm trusting you with him. Make sure he gets to Purgatory without harm. And God help you if you try to chain him up." I point my finger at her, trying to sound like the voice of authority, but my words don't come out as strong as I hoped. I sound like a whiney teenager pouting because her best friend is moving away.

Levi's tongue lolls out of the side of his mouth. He is silently laughing at me. His misplaced humor slaps the steel back into my spine.

Mandy nods and then drops to her knee, with her right arm crossing her chest in a bow. Others follow. It is completely mortifying.

"Get up," I hiss. Although I expected that at the fort, I really don't want them kneeling before me in this manner. I am not a queen. And I certainly am not a god. I am just me, and with the audience in the house behind me, this show of loyalty is embarrassing.

They rise with creases between their eyes and unsure expressions on their faces.

"I know I demanded it back in York, but we are beyond that." I take a deep breath and glance over the crowd. Even though it would have settled my nerves, I don't send my radar out to see whether there were dissenters in the pack. I meet Mandy's gaze, still feeling antsy about the plan. "I trust in you to do the right thing for this world."

Weighty words and they have the desired effect. The reapers nod, and Mandy reaches out to grab Levi's collar.

I swallow, wishing I could just wrap my arms around his neck in a goodbye hug, but that is not possible. I don't know if it will ever be.

When the reapers dissolve in the air, along with Levi, my eyes blur from the sudden mist of tears.

Chapter 6

"YOU DID THE RIGHT thing," my mother says from the backseat of the car as we pass under the Welcome to Maine sign on the Piscataqua River Bridge on Interstate 95.

I glance out the window at the passing scenery. I miss Levi already. His sideways humor always brings me back from the edge of a dark abyss. Exhaustion racks my bones, and my stomach growls as loud as Levi.

My father gives my arm a pat and focuses back on the road as he hangs back from the rest of the pack of cars traveling from the lake house.

"I'm still all confused about what just happened," Zane says. "I thought the reapers weren't on our side?"

"The ones that remain seem to be, but they left their post for long enough for Heaven to get some assassins to our side." My father turns the blinker on and takes a different road, peeling away from the rest of the crowd. He glances at the rearview mirror. "What's your address?" he asks Zane.

My stomach lurches. "No, Dad." I don't want to put Zane in that position. Especially when we don't have Levi with us to intervene if Zane's father steps out of line.

"Your father is right, especially if there are assassins on the loose already. 213 Birch Hill Road," Zane says. "You'll be safer there. Besides, if you can control an angel descendant, you can control an asshole human."

I glance in the backseat, barely making out Zane in the shadows. "I don't think this is a good idea." If his father comes at him, I know I wouldn't hesitate to strike him dead on the spot, especially after seeing the condition Zane was in on Thanksgiving.

"I won't let anything happen," my father says. "If he so much as flinches in Zane's direction, I'll lay him out flat."

"That's if he's even there," Zane says under his breath as the car crosses over the highway to the west side of the town.

I rarely come over this way. This is the poorest section of York. To the north is Mount Agamenticus and the rolling estates leading to it. The shoreline has the same air of wealth. Just like Papa's home, there were gated estates, but as we continue, the modest homes turn to a collection of farms and nothing bigger than double-wide trailer homes. They are larger than some of the run-down summer cottages on the shoreline, but they seem more worn, if that's possible. Maybe it's just the darkness creeping in around us that makes them look that way.

When my father turns in to the driveway of a small single-level home, I blink at it and swallow the pity that wells up. I live a charmed life on an estate by the sea. This is a landlocked home next to a quarry. Everything around it is covered in a fine gray dust, making it look almost ghostly in quality.

Zane sits up straighter in the car and his jaw goes rigid. "My truck is gone," he says in almost a growl. "The asshole took my truck!"

"Well, we have Faith's car," my father says as he rolls to a stop, and then turns the car off.

67

"The difference is you intend to give the car back." Zane gets out of the car and heads to the front door. He leans down and picks up a rock under the bush, and a moment later, has a key in his hand. Even he has a hide-a-key.

I press my lips against a smile as we all get out of the car and follow him. He doesn't seem to be in the mood for any ribbing, so I keep my humor to myself.

Zane pauses with the key in the door, as if he's having second thoughts. The lost look in his eyes makes me want to reach out and touch him, to reassure him that whatever lay beyond the door wouldn't change my feelings.

"This isn't what you are accustomed to." He glances back at me.

"It will be fine," my father says before I can say the same. He puts his arm around my mother and gives her a squeeze. "Right?"

She rolls her eyes. "Nick's right. It can't be any worse than our friend Noah's house in Florida. That place was barely standing. If a stiff wind came along, we were always afraid the walls were going to collapse on us."

Something about the way she says it seems to soothe whatever doubts Zane has because he swings the door open and reaches for the light switch on the inside wall. He flicks it a couple more times in frustration.

"Shit." He looks back at us with more aggravation written in the creases on his forehead and the low drop of his eyebrows. "Do any of you have a flashlight?"

I turn on my phone and flip the flashlight on. I went to hand it to Zane and my brain catches up to my actions before disaster strikes. I yank the phone away before Zane takes it from my hand. Scolding myself, I hand the phone to my father. "Can you give him this?" I nearly slam the phone in his palm.

I don't know if touching such a small thing at the same time will harm his soul, but I am not taking any chances.

My father does as I request with an eye roll and we follow Zane into the dark house. Zane stands in the empty living room—devoid of furniture, devoid of anything hinting at the fact people had lived there—just staring at the nothingness as he turns the light in all directions.

I wish there was enough light in the room to see his expression because the waves of conflicting emotions he's broadcasting wash over me in continuous succession. The overhead light in the kitchen flickers on.

Zane spins toward it with wide eyes, like he expects Levi to leap out of the cabinets or something. He glances at me.

"Did you just do that?"

Truthfully, I'm not sure, but I had wished for light and I guess that's the only light in the vicinity that's still here. "I wanted light because I could feel you freaking out. So, probably?" I shrug.

He gives me a nod and heads down the hallway with the phone light, leaving us in the stark kitchen light.

My father crosses to the refrigerator and opens it. Not even a crumb remains. It's like the Grinch had paid a visit while Zane was at our place. The freezer is just as barren. No dishes or glasses grace the cabinet shelves either.

Zane's face says it all as he slowly comes back down the hall to where we all wait. In the living room, he sits on the faded carpet and tosses my phone a few feet away. When he buries his face in his hands, I step toward him and stop, grinding my teeth together at my lack of being able to comfort him. He stays that way—his elbows on his knees and his hands covering his face—while his breath wheezes out from beneath his palms.

I want to string up his father. The asshole stripped the place barren and ran like the coward he is. My guess and probably Zane's as well is the bastard took off in a hurry when Zane didn't come home. Who knows, he's probably in Canada by now.

70

My mother approaches him because I can't console him the way I'd like to. She kneels next to him and places her hand on his back, rubbing it slowly. He stiffens, but she doesn't speak. She doesn't need to. Zane's loss weighs on the air like the thick Maine fog.

When he finally looks up, his tear-stained eyes meet mine. "He took everything I had," he says with such bitterness that I shiver. "That bastard thought I was dead and ran with everything. My truck. My equipment that I've spent years collecting. He even found where I had stashed my cash in my bedroom. Everything I've built... Gone." He closes his eyes and shakes his head. "I don't even have clothes besides what was in my backpack at your house." He waves in my direction. "And it isn't even Monday yet," he adds as he rakes his hand through his hair.

"You will be fine," my mother says.

Zane glances at her. "You're in the same boat as I am," he points out. "At least I still have my wallet and the measly hundred dollars that I keep as pocket change. But you two look like teenagers and right now, you've got no home, no clothing except what you are wearing right now, and I'd venture to guess money isn't something you've ever needed before. So, telling me it's going to be fine is pretty comical, considering."

My mother's hand stops moving on his back and her gaze jumps to my father's in that deer in the headlights manner, as if she is just now grasping what being alive truly means.

"Where do you think he went?" I ask.

"Probably Mexico. He has always hated the cold." Zane wipes his face and stands up, crossing into the kitchen. He pushes the lever for water, and nothing comes out. He bangs it down again. "We can't stay here."

"Why not?" my father asks.

"No water, no electricity, no heat." Zane stares at him as if he's daft.

My father points at the empty fireplace. "I saw wood out back, right?"

Zane glances at the fireplace with a sigh. "No matches or paper for kindling." He looks back at my father.

"I'm sure we can find something to light a fire with." My father crosses his arms, challenging Zane with an eyebrow raise.

"Dude, there's no food. No water. No toilet paper." He shrugs with his palms up.

"Look, this is the safest place for Missy. No one knows where you live. Not the Ryans, not the reapers, and not the angels. If you are so concerned about roughing it, you said you had a hundred dollars. Order a pizza and we can pick

72

it up and grab sodas, water, napkins, and matches at the same time. And toilet paper, if that's such an issue." My father makes an exaggerated eye roll.

"I have money at home. I can pay you back," I add, just to ease his mind. I don't want him to panic about money. Not while I'm living under the roof of one of the wealthiest men in America.

"Fine, but I don't have a phone."

"Use mine." I point to the phone still shining a light on the ceiling. He picks it up and shows me the lock screen before he puts it down and slides it across the floor to me. It comes close, and I lean over and swipe it off the ground. The local pizza place is practically on speed dial and with a couple of swipes of my finger, I hit the call button. "What kind of pizza do you all want?"

"Hawaiian," both Zane and my mother say.

"Hamburger," my father says a beat later.

Well, at least Zane and my mother have exemplary taste in pizza toppings. Although a hamburger pizza doesn't sound all that bad. My stomach growls again and I order two large pizzas and an extra-small Hawaiian, so we don't run out. At the pace my stomach seems to be devouring my insides, I could probably suck down an entire pizza by myself.

"They said twenty minutes." I slide my phone into my back pocket.

"I'll drive," my father says and offers Zane a hand to help him off the floor.

I can tell Zane isn't all that thrilled with the prospect of being alone with my father. I open my mouth and my mother interrupts me.

"We'll stay here and figure out what we can scrounge in the way of wood and kindling based on what's in the yard. Okay?"

"Seems reasonable to me," my father answers. He didn't even wait for Zane. He starts toward the door and glances back.

I send a seething glare at him, purposely narrowing my eyes. I'm not sure I want him alone with the guy I'm... I suddenly realize I don't know the status of what we are. Friends? Girlfriend-boyfriend? I'm not sure what to even refer to him as besides his name. Regardless of our precarious status, I do want to hear from Zane. "Is that okay with you? Because if it isn't, I can go."

"I'll be fine," Zane says, but he does not follow with the same enthusiasm. "But there isn't anything here. I've already looked."

"We'll just do another once-over and see if we can at least get the water on. Now go." My mother makes a shooing motion toward the door.

We watch from the entryway as the car pulls out of the driveway and my mother closes the door and turns to me.

"You have the ability to conjure things." It wasn't a question, especially when her gaze dropped to the lovely knife holder I created for Heaven's blade.

"So?"

"So, turn on the water, just like you turned on this light, so we can at least go to the bathroom. And while you're at it, conjure up some sleeping bags and pillows." She points at the empty floor.

My skin suddenly itches uncomfortably at the orders she utters, and I shift in place. "Is this what you did?"

"When I needed to, yes."

"So, this is more Fate's powers rather than Death's?"

"No. Your father could conjure things much easier than I ever could. But I learned over the years. By the time you came along, I could conjure whatever I wanted to wear or however I felt like having my hair on any day. Or if I needed a weapon, and it wasn't hidden away

75

wherever Kylee hides things, I'd wish it out of the ether and voila." She spreads her arms like a goddess used to getting her way.

I had difficulty with my first outfit, but since then I hadn't had any missteps. I glance at the floor and bite my lower lip, debating. "How many sleeping bags?" I finally ask. I don't want to assume they'll sleep separately, even though I'd feel a hell of a lot more comfortable that way.

She chews on her nail as she studies the floor.

I can almost hear her internal dialog arguing for and against one sleeping bag. Silently, I wish for separate to be the answer because just the thought of my mother and father going at it in the same room makes me puke in my mouth a little.

"I don't think either of you will want to hear our shenanigans, so four would work."

Oh, hell no. Four sleeping bags and four pillows it is. I close my eyes, envisioning those sleeping bags that were used to keep warm in the arctic. A cool flow of air seems to breeze through me like I'm not solid flesh and bone. It's the same feeling I got when I pulled this outfit successfully together. When I open my eyes, four bags stretch out on the floor, as if an invisible hand unrolled them at my bidding. I smile and glance at my mother.

She just nods her approval and I concentrate on pillows.

I like mine soft and fluffy, so everyone is going to have to deal with that. Fluffy pillows that match the deep green of the sleeping bags appear on the openings of the bags.

I turn to my mother, feeling very accomplished by the magic that tickles my mind.

She points toward the sink. "Think you can turn on the water and the electricity and keep it on for a couple of days?"

That isn't quite as easy as conjuring something I can envision, like sleeping bags or clothes. That's a mechanical process, and I don't know if I can just wish running water through the house or not. The light had been a fluke. I wanted to see Zane's face and the only overhead light in the place happened to come on at the same time.

I decide to tackle electricity first because I don't think trying to do them at the same time is a really sane choice. Now, if I had a death wish, that might be a feat worth performing. But considering I don't want to die anytime soon, I cross to the wall and gather up every bit of my science know-how and put my hands near the light switches.

Electricity must have a signature of some kind, since it is just a mass of energy moving from one place to another. I close my eyes and take a deep breath, reaching for the energy.

It takes a few minutes to find any pulse, but I keep having to widen my search beyond the house until I find the source near the edge of the road running parallel to the house. My senses scan the source until I feel the underground wire that connects this house to the source. With a push, I clear the block the power company put in place, and the surge of energy that flows into my hands nearly knocks me across the room. The kitchen light flares bright and a couple of ceiling lights in the hallway come to life.

I catch myself before I pinwheel onto the floor and shake the sting out of my hands. I certainly don't want that same rush to happen when I try to do that to the water, otherwise every pipe in this house will burst. I am amazed that the surge didn't blow the electrical circuits.

My mother smiles at me, beaming like a proud parent.

I cross to the sink and push the lever to the open position. I stare at it for a moment. Maybe there's an easier way than using my magical skills. I glance down the hallway, wondering whether this one is as simple as turning on a valve. I head down the hall, trying each door as I pass. A closet. A bedroom. A bathroom. Then I finally find stairs that lead down. I flip on the light switch and grin as the light bathes the way.

The stairs are not rickety like most old houses and I'm thankful as I climb down them. I cross to where the water heater sits in the far corner. In Alex's house, there's a lever near their water system that turns off the water drawing from the city line.

My mother is close enough to make me nervous, and I glance back at her, raising an eyebrow. She moves a couple of steps back with a nod.

Starting at the water heater, I scan the pipes in the ceiling.

"What are you doing?"

"Looking for the valve to turn on the water." There are plenty of pipes overhead, but I'm looking for the one that goes through the basement wall. That's usually the one that has the turnoff valve on it, at least according to what Alex had told us when he was adding a bathroom in the downstairs family room area.

On the far side of the furnace, I catch a red-handled valve set to the off position. I'm glad I looked first because had I willed water to the house, it would have destroyed that valve. I crossed and stood under it on my tiptoes. Even jumping, I couldn't quite reach it. I don't even consider my mother. She's shorter than I am.

I glance around the barren basement, wishing for a darn step stool or ladder. Before me, the air shimmers and a three-step ladder appears, already open and waiting for me to climb up it.

I have to suppress a laugh. I really like this conjuring ability. I step up and turn the lever to the on position. The moment I do, the rush of running water reaches my ears.

I climb down and smile at my mother. "I didn't need to will that one after all."

She smiles back, with her eyes sparkling with pride. "I'm impressed. How did you know about that?" She waves at the valve.

"Alex does a lot of stuff around the house. He showed me where it was and explained that when they go away for any extended period, it's a good thing to turn off. Especially in the winter. It could save the pipes from bursting."

She follows me back upstairs.

"So, he doesn't just fix things with his mind?"

I laugh and shake my head. "No. And he wants us to be self-sufficient, so he tries to teach us the things he thinks are important. Like changing tires on a car or knowing where the water turnoff valves are in most houses."

"Hmm." We stop in the living room and she stares at the empty fireplace. "Care to conjure some wood for the fire?" she asks before I cross the room.

"There's wood out back. We can grab it after we eat." My muscles already feel strained, but I think some physical exercise of moving wood will actually help me sleep later.

I sit on the farthest sleeping bag, putting distance between me and the nearest bag, so I don't have any possibility of hitting anyone near me if I flail in my sleep. I rarely have nightmares, but this whole thing has me on edge enough to want to prevent a soul-sucking mistake.

As much as I find this conjuring stuff amazing, I'd trade it all to kiss Zane again.

"I'm sorry about Dad," I say after a moment. I haven't said anything to my mother since the jobs passed to me and I consumed my father's soul.

She takes a deep breath and gives me a sad smile. "You didn't know. Neither did we. Out of everyone there, I am glad it's your father. While he is off, if you know what I mean, he's not so far off from himself. It's hard to explain. He still is fiercely protective, and he still takes my hand when we are walking or puts his arm around me, although I think it's more out of habit than feeling." She sits down on the third sleeping bag, keeping her distance. "It could have been worse," she says, but I catch the way she averts her eyes.

"Why are you placating me?" I blurt.

She meets my gaze as her smile fades away. "I'm not. There are times he's more like his old self and then others when all his manners disappear. It's not consistent." She shrugs. "And there isn't anything we can do about it, so I'm choosing to live with the circumstances dealt to me and try to find the good in everything."

This is by far one of the longest conversations I think I have ever had with my mother, and I realize if we were in school together, we might have been friends because her inherently good view of the world is just so innocent. I don't know how, after all these years as a deity, she can still exude innocence.

I pray if the day ever comes that I must pass on the torch to someone else, that I'm as poised and wholesome as my mother.

Chapter 7

ZANE AND MY FATHER arrive with the pizzas, sodas, waters, paper plates, napkins, and a package of toilet paper. He drops the pies on the ground between the sleeping bags and heads down the hallway to the bathroom with the toilet paper.

When he returns, a crease between his eyes deepens. He crosses and takes a seat on the opposite side of my mother. As far away from me as possible. My father hadn't taken the spot next to me yet, so Zane's choice of where to sit has my curiosity climbing. Along with the fact of how skittish he seems to be acting.

I glance at my father as he takes the seat next to me. "What did you say to him in the car?"

My father opens his mouth to speak.

"He didn't say anything that hadn't already been said," Zane says. It takes him a few moments to actually look at me, as if I'm something to be feared.

I glance back at my father. "Seriously, what did you say?"

"I told him that if it had been anyone else in that house who you touched, they wouldn't just have had their soul sucked out of them, they would have died." He breaks open the seals on the pizza boxes and flips the tops open one by one, setting them toward the foot of the sleeping bags in the middle of us all. "You are Death," he adds when I just gawk at him. "That comes with curses all its own. And you have about as much control over that as I had."

"You didn't die." I reach for the untouched pizza. If no one else is going to dig in, I will. My stomach has been rumbling since before we left for the lake house and I had exercised a lot of magic in these few hours. I need to replenish my energy.

"No. But I think that's because we were technically dead when you stripped us of our roles. I probably should be dead right now, but I think it kind of backfired because you brought us back to life."

"But you didn't kill me when you became Death," my mother says as she reaches for pizza, too, except she uses one of the paper plates Zane dropped on the floor near our bedding.

"I had the benefit of a warning from my father. I knew my touch was deadly unless I wrapped those I cared about in a protective cocoon. You and Noah were protected because I willed it."

"Wouldn't that be the same with him?" I wave at Zane and dug into my pizza. "If you could will your touch not to be deadly, couldn't I will my touch not to suck out his soul?"

"I don't know the limits of your power," he says. "I could never bring someone back to life by sheer will. I had to turn back the clock to do that."

My mother turns her head and stares at my father.

"You knew I did that," my father says to her questioning eyes. "And then I screwed up by giving you the book of Fates to hold on to. I could instill ideas into people too, just like I've got control over fire and water." He glances at the fireplace. "Or had those powers before Missy took the helm. But back to the here and now. I never could raise the dead at will, or eviscerate reapers, either." He looks straight at me. "Neither of those powers were in our wheelhouse before."

Just as Zane reaches for the pizza, the front door bursts open.

I am on my feet, facing the intruder, before my brain catches up. Zane is on his feet too, his pizza cast aside carelessly.

"You!" The man points at Zane, and the stench of bourbon fills the room.

"Where's my stuff?" Zane says as he squares his feet, waiting. Every muscle in his body is visibly tense and just waiting for the first fist to fly.

It's as if the man doesn't even see the rest of us in the room. "You were supposed to die out there," he growls and then charges at Zane, hitting him full out like a linebacker.

Zane goes down with a heartbreaking thud. His head bounces against the floor.

My feet move as fury fills every cell.

I don't care that I can strip this bastard of either his soul or his life. He is hurting Zane, and all I can feel is the burn of retribution.

My father is faster. He tackles Zane's father, ripping him away from Zane and throwing him to the ground. My dad isn't large by any means, but he is scrappy as hell.

I want to help Zane, but I just point my mother to him instead. I cross as Zane's father climbs to his feet with the sourest expression I've ever seen scrunching his ugly face. I guess Zane must have gotten his good looks from his mother because this man isn't even in the same stratosphere as Zane.

I shove my father aside and block access to Zane as I will my scythe into existence. The blade glistens in the light, casting its deadly intent to everyone in the room.

"Do you know who I am?" I pound the blunt end of my weapon on the floor to get his attention. The charm on my wrist dings and a chill skitters through me, especially when the knowledge of the name listed flows into me.

His father reaches inside his shirt and pulls out a gun.

I am not allowing that entry to come to fruition. Before the bastard can raise the gun to take aim, I bring the business end of my scythe sweeping down as fast as a bolt of lightning.

His severed hand holding the gun drops to the ground, where it can no longer do any harm.

Blood spurts from the clean stump of his wrist and Zane's father blinks a few times before the pain renders a wail. He grips his arm above the bloody stump.

"Missy, don't." Zane's shaking voice comes from behind me.

"He beat you practically to death," I say, but I don't dare take my eyes off the shrieking man messing up the floor with his blood. Can I protect this idiot from my powers? The thought flits through my mind, changing him from a sure kill, to my first test subject. "Besides, I want to see if I can control my powers."

"Who the fuck are you?" he screams at me.

I smile and step forward.

"He may be an asshole, but he's the only family I've got," Zane says.

Now I do glance over my shoulder at Zane. He pulls his hand away from the back of his head. Blood smears the soft skin of his palm.

Darkness fills me, along with the need to enact justice. It pounds in my temples like a freight train. Seeing Zane bloody again is all I need to test my hypothesis out. I stalk forward, willing protection around the asshole from both my deadly touch as well as the soul-stealing ability. I grab his good arm.

He stiffens, and his eyes widen. His cries of pain hitch in his chest just before the room goes white. This time, his soul rips from his body with such force, the tearing of it sounds like wet flesh being torn apart. His soul is not the white light I expect—it's yellowing as if it's diseased—and I recoil from the sight just before it slams into my chest, absorbing into my skin whether or not I want it to.

His soul is as black and evil as I imagined Lucifer's was. A vile taste fills my mouth, and I nearly gag at the essence of the man. He does not have an ounce of any redemptive quality in his heart, and he hates Zane with a passion that creates a loathing in me I abhor.

This man hates that he was saddled with a spawn he didn't have any party in creating.

The transfer only takes a few seconds, but when the light dies down, I stare into his still living eyes. Eyes now devoid of a soul. His eyes are wide, as if he is seeing me for the first time, and I catch a hint of fear blooming there.

I'm not proud, but that fear gives me a hint of satisfaction. I'm glad this bastard has an inkling that his lousy existence is about to be snuffed out. I am just sad he isn't going on to Hell to live through the same pain and fear that Zane dealt with daily.

My willing him safe didn't save him from my curse. It only saved him from Death's touch. But that is about to change. "I revoke my protection," I snarl.

He wheezes a rattling breath as his good hand flies to his chest. As efficiently as I had sucked his soul from his body, I recklessly stomp the life out of him. I let go of the husk of a man and he crumples to the ground in an ashen-colored heap.

"You just killed my father!"

I turn to see both my father and mother holding Zane back. The horrifying taste in my mouth increases. Zane cared for this bastard, despite all the horrible things he did over the years.

"He came here to kill you."

"You don't know that," he growls as tears cascade down his handsome face.

I will the Book of Fates into existence and stare at the name I knew had been scribed in the book. I inhale and glance down at the shriveled carcass without an ounce of regret before turning toward Zane with the book facing him.

The name Zane Bradley is scrawled across the screen.

Zane pales and meets my gaze.

"I made a choice." I will not apologize for choosing him over the loser on the floor, and when I turn the book back around toward me, the name morphs from Zane's name to his father's. "I was not willing to let that cold-hearted bastard kill you. He wasn't even your real father." I will both my weapon and the Book of Fates back into the charms on my bracelet. The weight of them seems a little heavier this time. After all, I had taken a human life. I had committed an atrocious sin.

I turn toward the corpse; we can't have him stinking up the place and we really have nowhere else that is this safe to hide out. Lifting my hands, I will the body into a fine dust that I force up and out of the chimney and into the cool night air.

I dust my hands on my thighs and then, without a word, I cross and sit back down, focusing on the pizza and ignoring the open-mouthed stares of all three of them. I need something to wash out the vile taste of his soul from the back of my throat.

My parents let go of him and settle back down on the sleeping bags, as if nothing horrific had just happened. I guess it really isn't for them. After being Death and Fate for so long, the shock of human indecency doesn't seem to faze them the way it's throwing me.

"What do you mean, he isn't my real father?" Zane finally takes a seat, slower to return to the pizza feast than the rest of us. In fact, he pushes his plate away.

He still looks pale and I'm not sure it's because he just witnessed someone's death. Worry creeps under the hardened crust I built to deal with my actions. "How bad is the cut on his head?" I nod toward him and my mother goes to take a look.

She winces as she moved some of his hair aside. Her fingers come out of his hair smeared with red streaks. "I think you might need stitches."

"I'm okay." Zane brushes her away. "I just need a wet towel or something to use as a compress and a little soda."

I blink at him and glance up at my mother. She shakes her head, silently telling me it's worse than just a little cut. I will some liquid bandage into her hand. Her eyebrows shoot up at the little vial of liquid she now holds.

"She's going to fix you up, so hold still," I say and nod to my mother.

Zane glances over his shoulder at her and then back toward me.

"Stop ignoring my question."

92

He winces as my mother parts his hair with her fingers and applies a line of the adhesive to the cut.

"Hold still," she says and seems to press the edges of the cut together.

"Tell me what you meant," he directs at me through clenched teeth.

Zane has a right to know. "He isn't your biological father."

"How the fuck do you know that?" He shoos my mother away and then reaches for a paper cup and one of the bottles of soda.

"You tend to get a huge download of information about someone when you absorb their soul. Although I could do without his. It's awful and I wish I had just killed him so he could have an eternity atoning for his sins." I put the pizza down, no longer hungry.

Zane pours himself a glass of soda and then pours me one, pushing mine toward me instead of handing it to me. That small gesture warms the chill right out of me. It also tightens my throat.

My hand shakes as I reach for the cup. The adrenaline finally fades and my horrible actions hit home. Tears fill my eyes and my chin quivers. "I killed him."

Zane goes to move toward me, as if he wants to still protect me from the pain those three words create.

I put my hand up to stop him. "It's my sin to bear, not yours," I whisper as hot tears spill down my cheeks. "I'll be fine."

I don't want him to touch me. It isn't safe, and God knows I want him, of all people, to be safe.

I'd just need to learn to breathe through this crippling dread on my own.

LONG AFTER THE FIRE Dad and Zane built in the fireplace turned to embers and my mother and father's snoring filled the space, I tire of staring at the ceiling as my mind continuously relives my mistake. Although I can't really categorize it as a true mistake. At least now I know my protections only apply to letting someone continue breathing. I imagine the results if I had tried that on someone I care about. That leaves me more restless and intent on protecting those I love.

I climb to my feet and find the door that leads to the backyard. A weathered picnic table sits in the open yard, and I cross and stretch out on the top. The deep, clear night surrounds me, sending a chill around me as comforting as a wet blanket.

The vast galaxy shimmers across the moonless sky, uninhibited by any streetlight.

The creak of the door makes me tilt my head back to see who else can't sleep. Zane crosses and takes a seat on the bench. He stares at me and bites his lower lip.

"I should be angry with you."

I just nod, because he has the right. After all, I killed his only known family, even if he was a major dick.

"I'm not." He crosses his arms on the table and props his chin on his hand. "The longer I think about it, the more I wish you had filleted him with your scythe."

I raise my eyebrow at him.

"I know. Sick, right?"

I glance back at the sky. "It's not like the thought didn't cross my mind."

His audible sigh reaches my ears, and I glance at him again. "You have no idea how much I just want to climb on top of you and kiss you right now." He smiles in a way that flushes my entire body. "Among other things." But instead of doing just that, he stretches out on the picnic table seat and stares up at the cosmos with me.

"Even with what I did today?"

He doesn't answer and my stomach flips. If what I did alienates him, I'm not sure I can deal with that. I roll onto my side, peering down at him. He just continues staring at the stars above like they have answers we need. His gaze moves to mine.

"It hurts not being able to hold you. Weird, huh?" He attempts a light laugh, but it falls flat. "I needed you earlier. I needed your arms around me." He shakes his head and studies my face. "And it hurt worse than my head not to be able to hold you. Hell, the more time I spend with you, the less I seem to care about whether or not I have a soul."

He reaches up to touch my face.

My heart slams a panicked beat and I move away fast enough to jab my ass into a sliver of wood sticking up from the table. I stop the wince from hissing from between my teeth. That would be a surefire way to bring Zane right into my arms. Or worse, have him insist on getting the sliver out.

I cannot strip him of his soul. Not with how much his heart bleeds through his every word. If he didn't have a soul, I would not have fallen for him the way I have—hard.

As far as the sliver went, I'd have to have my father take it out with some tweezers later so it doesn't fester into something that could land me in the hospital. Although mortifying, it is still better than making a hospital full of the morally corrupt.

"So, what's next?" he asks, but his voice has an edge to it, one that my actions created.

I slowly lay back and search the constellations. I don't have an answer that would ease his mind. I am going up against Heaven, and if I die, the world dies. But there aren't any palatable alternatives.

"I could take one of the roles," he says quietly. "Then Heaven wouldn't have you on their hit list."

"No." He needs to have a life, even if it's without me. "You will die."

"You didn't." He sits up and rests his elbows on the table.

"I'm not..." I look away.

"Normal?" He chuckles. "Thank the fucking stars for that."

I glance at him. He's starting to sound a lot like my father in the loose language department. "No. I wasn't supposed to be. Levi called me an enigma."

"Well, you are, and you are now some sort of mystical immortal. One with a much kinder heart than mine."

"Excuse me?"

"I would have made my father suffer." He meets my stare. "I would have escorted him to Hell myself."

"I needed a test subject," I say, defending my actions. "I needed to know if I could safeguard someone from losing their soul and I saw an opportunity."

He rolls his eyes. "I'm not judging you. Don't go getting all defensive on me." He reaches out again, but this time he stops on his own, pulling his hand back and clenching it into a fist. He pounds the table. "Goddammit all." He gets up and heads back into the house, muttering under his breath about life being unfair and all.

I realize with a sick certainty that I need to get away from Zane. I am more lethal to him than I am to anyone else.

I want to be in his arms.

I want to feel his body against me, and not just spooning in bed like the other night.

I want more, and the longer I am around him, the deeper he gets under my skin. If I stay, he will be soulless in a matter of days.

Chapter 8

THIS TIME, I WAIT until I hear three distinct snores and then I go out the front door as quietly as humanly possible. I need to hone my skills, and I need to get away from any more mistakes. Zane is safe with my parents.

I walk to the end of the driveway and look toward home. Yearning pulls my midsection that way, but I turn and trudge in the opposite direction, putting time and distance between me and Zane's house. In the wee hours of the night, I blend in with the woods surrounding me.

I know I need to find somewhere to sleep, but I can't stop while I'm still in Maine.

Just as the sky lightens with dawn, the air shimmers next to me. Mandy appears by my side.

I stop, and she takes a couple of steps before she stops, too.

"Why are you here?" I ask and then, as my brain fog clears, I add, "And where is Levi?"

"He's fine. He's happily devouring whatever tries to come into Purgatory."

"So, if he's okay, why are you here?"

Mandy looks down and then back up at me as she shifts from foot to foot. She reaches into her pocket and pulls out a folded piece of paper. "Well, one of the angels got by him and spared me so I could give you this." She reluctantly hands it to me.

I use the tips of my fingernails to take the note, but instead of opening it and reading what an angel from Heaven has to say, I am more concerned about Mandy's comment.

"How many did the angel not spare?"

Mandy winces. "I think there may be less than a hundred of us left."

I blink and slowly drop to the ground. I didn't even feel them go. I should have. Mandy crouches down, her face transforming through the tears filling my eyes.

"You...you care about us?" Her voice cracks and she reaches out to touch me.

"Don't," I snap, and she freezes in place. "Don't touch me. I'm cursed, and I don't want to harm you."

She slowly pulls her hand back. "You care?"

I let out a high-pitch laugh. "Of course, I care. Why would you think I don't?"

"Well, you annihilated more than half of us."

Point taken. I close my eyes and hang my head. "They wanted to do harm to my family." I open my eyes. "I know you weren't party to what happened. If you were, you would not be here. I'm sorry I wasn't there to help you fend off the angels that got by Levi."

She glances off into the distance. "I don't know if you can survive their smiting."

I'm not sure either, but I have a host of allies who harbor angel fire. And they had toasted an archangel with it in the past. But even so, they haven't had to fight a host of angels from Heaven.

"And how did you survive?"

She winces and stands, glancing at the road. "They promised to spare me if I brought them through to this realm."

My senses itch, and I stare up at her before I glance around for the ambush that seems imminent. "Where are they?"

"Read the note." She points to the nearly forgotten paper in my hand.

I open it and stare at the scrawl.

You have sentenced the world to death by not heeding our warning. You are an abomination that cannot exist and will be terminated by Heaven's might.

Those who stand with you are just as damned as you are.

As punishment for your sin, we promise each and every one of those who stand by you and those who you stole from our grip will endure an eternity of torture alone.

We promise none of you will see each other ever again.

My chest tightens and I slowly look up at Mandy as I climb to my feet. "And you are standing with Heaven?"

She shakes her head. "But some are. Most of us scattered when we got here. Especially since we don't look like reapers anymore. We have a chance of blending in and hiding from their wrath."

I glance at the note again. "Can you get Levi and bring him back without getting hurt?"

"No. They left guards."

My heart pounds and I narrow my eyes, studying her. "Levi isn't okay, is he?" There was no way short of him being chained again that he would ever allow angels through. Not under his watch.

She glances at the ground. "When they couldn't smite him, they caged him."

"Why did you lie to me before?" I hiss the words out and refrain from grabbing her.

A pair of headlights approach, making me step into the grass and nod for Mandy to follow. The truck slows to a stop, and Zane glances out the passenger window at the two of us. He lifts my cell phone.

"Holly texted."

He doesn't need to say anything more. The glare he gives me says everything. I abandoned him and there is no level of forgiveness in his eyes.

"Where are my parents?" I ask as I stare at the decal on the passenger side door. This is Zane's truck. I hadn't even noticed it in the driveway when I left. That explains how his father came barreling in like a wrecking ball last night.

"They went to Papa's house. Everyone is there." He glances at Mandy. "Why is she here?"

I wave the note in my hand. "There's been a breach." I open the passenger door and step aside to allow Mandy to get into the backseat.

"She can walk," Zane says, pulling my attention back to him. "We have some things to discuss."

That's the last thing I need, but I give Mandy a nod, knowing she doesn't really need a lift to wherever we are going. She probably wants to go off and blend in as she was saying, and I don't blame her for wanting a last hurrah before the worlds as we know them end.

Zane does not take me to Papa's house. Instead of driving by his house, he pulls in and leaves me in the truck, slamming the front door behind him with a bang. I wait for him to come back, and when he doesn't, I think about driving myself, but he has the car keys.

I climb out of the truck and with every step closer to the house, dread wraps another frigid finger around my heart. He stands by the

104

fireplace with his arms on the mantel, just staring down at the embers in the hearth.

I close the door behind me and his entire back tenses. He turns and stalks toward me like he wants to shake sense into me. I press my back against the door, trying to literally push my way through it. When Zane's hands slam into the wood on either side of my head, I gasp. He leans close enough for me to feel the heat and anger radiating from his skin.

"Please don't," I whisper. My chin quivers.

"Why not? You don't seem to give a damn about me."

Hot tears spill over and run down my cheeks. I don't dare move. I want to push him away and call him a pig-headed fool. I want to bridge the slight distance between us and crush his lips with mine. Damn him, I want his arms around me.

"I care too much." I meet his wild-eyed glare. "It's only a matter of time before..." More tears spill over. "Before we..." I can't finish the sentence. "I'm not that strong, and I can't protect you," I finally sputter. "This hurts me just as much as it hurts you."

He pushes back and takes a step away to give us both some breathing room. "That's not a good enough reason to leave in the dead of night."

"Yes. It is. You would do the same damn thing if you were in my shoes," I yell, moving as close as I dare. "You would do anything to protect me if the roles were reversed. Even if it meant leaving." Tears blur my vision, and I run my hands through my hair. "And now everything is going to shit, anyway." I throw the note onto the floor between us and step back against the door as sobs rip from my chest. "They smited most of the reapers, and Levi has been caged by the asshole angels somewhere in Purgatory, so there is no one holding them back." I swipe at my face as he picks up the letter and reads it.

He pales as Heaven's horrifying promises of wiping us all out are outlined in gruesome detail. "They would do this?" He waves the letter. "These are supposed to be the good guys. Why would they slaughter your whole family?"

"To break me." It is simple, and it is working.

Chapter 9

HE DRIVES SLOWLY, AS if he doesn't want us to arrive in time to see whatever slaughter is coming. Without Levi blocking the gates, they are free to swarm the reaper realm and slip into ours. The thought terrifies me.

"What did Holly say?"

Zane remains quiet and tosses me my phone. This grand, silent treatment is grating on my nerves. He never admitted he would have done the same thing, either. He refuses to acknowledge the danger of coming with me. And he would not let me go alone to the house, not with the possibility of the world ending tonight.

But he also wasn't going to stop me from coming home and making sure my family was safe. So here we are, in the truck. Me with my arms crossed in the passenger seat and him giving me this damn attitude.

I pick up my phone and swipe the text app open, finding Holly's text. She asked whether I was okay. And there isn't just one text. There are a dozen of them trying to get me to answer, each one increasingly frantic until she finally called. "What did you tell her?"

"That you were sleeping and would call her when you woke up. I told her we were fine."

I glance out the passenger side window with that lump permanently lodged in my throat. I swallow, blinking away the mist that springs over my vision. I take a few moments to catch my voice. "Thank you," I finally squeak out.

He grunts. Both his hands grip the steering wheel to the point his knuckles turn white. The muscles in his jaw stand out like he's clenching his teeth. Everything about him is as tight as a coiled snake ready to strike.

"What?"

"You're walking into a trap."

"What choice do I have?"

"Let me take one of the roles. That way, they have no beef with you. Either give me the book or give me the scythe."

"There is no guarantee that it will work. You saw me try to pass it back to my father."

He sends a searing stare in my direction before looking back at the road. "I have a soul."

"I cannot risk your life on a maybe. If I'm touching the scythe at the same time, there's no guarantee I won't strip you of your soul and kill you. I'm not losing you that way."

"You can bring me back." He glances at me.

"I don't know how to do that without a damn portal. And don't say I brought my parents back from the dead because I don't have the foggiest clue how that happened."

"If they kill you, we all die."

"I don't intend on dying by their filthy hands. Besides, if we all die, then we all pass on together."

"Not according to that note." He points to the paper on the console between us.

Heaven not only swore the Deaths of all who stood by me—which meant everyone who attended Thanksgiving at Papa's house—but every being I brought back from the dead. They also promised each and every one of us would be ushered through the gates of Hell for an eternity on the racks, with no chance of ever getting off.

Basically, if I don't give myself up freely, none of us would ever see each other again.

"It's total bullshit," I mutter under my breath. They are hoping they'll scare me to the point I won't be able to see straight. But on the other side, I am in control. Purgatory is my domain, and they killed my federation.

I can feel my blood pressure rising, along with the anger rushing to the surface and drowning out all remnants of fear. They are screwing with the wrong girl.

What had Tom Ryan said earlier?

Angels are dicks.

If the angels try to smite me, that will be their last mistake. I really believe I am not smitable. Not with the incredible power flowing through my veins. Not with the absolute uniqueness I bring to the table. Not with the ability to turn reapers to ash. And from the wrath and spite outlined in their note, I am ready for a bloody battle.

I am prepared to strip every one of those bastards of their souls before I blow them into oblivion with Heaven's blade. That's my secret surprise. They have no clue I possess the ultimate weapon. Although my scythe can do damage, Heaven's blade will blink them out of existence like it did to Lucifer.

I have years of self-defense lessons, and I know how to handle multiple attacks, especially multiples with weapons. That was Papa's favorite test for obtaining a black belt, and I moved fast enough through my forms to impress the entire family. I just need to keep control of Heaven's blade throughout the battle, and not end up nicking myself in the mayhem.

That kind of mistake would snap me, and probably the rest of humanity, right out of existence. It is also the reason I had to face the angels alone. I can't take a chance of scratching anyone who is on my side of the equation.

That's my plan.

I take a shaky breath. But the boy driving the car will never let me go out to the battlefield alone. The only reason he let me go before was Levi, and I no longer have the benefit of Levi to protect my back.

"I can't let you go up against Heaven alone."

It's like he read my mind. I mop my face as we turn onto Papa's road. I have no idea how to make him understand. "You have to. Otherwise, I will be powerless."

He slams the brakes, and the seat belt tightens from my forward momentum. "Despite what it looks like, I can fight." He turns hard eyes in my direction.

"I will have Heaven's blade. If I get moving too fast and not paying attention to where you are, I could slice you into oblivion."

"You can't fight." He laughed.

"What? Because I'm a girl?" I glare at him, and he has the audacity to shrug. "I will have you know, I'm a second-degree black belt. If I could touch you right now, I'd kick your ass just for laughing at me."

"That still doesn't mean you have actual fighting experience," he says.

"Being someone's punching bag doesn't qualify as fighting experience, either." I know the moment the words slip out of my mouth I should never have uttered them. But now that they were out, I can't take it back.

He presses his lips together and the muscle in his jaw jumps. The truck moves slowly forward as he lifts his foot off the brake. We are back to the silent treatment, and this time, I don't think I can break through his purposeful barrier so easily.

"Damn it, Zane," I whisper and look out the window at the sun breaching the horizon, bathing us with a new and uncertain dawn.

114

Chapter 10

PAPA'S DRIVEWAY IS AS crowded as I had ever seen it. Zane pulls up alongside the gate on the road outside instead of blocking everyone in. I open the gate and step inside, hitting the button to reengage it as soon as we are clear. We walk down the driveway in silence, but a noise like crunching leaves under a boot behind us makes me glance over my shoulder.

An angel is coming at us with a feral grin on her face. Her skin glows, reminding me of when Papa had gone all angelic on his brother. The gate slams closed behind the winged being, emitting a sound that I had grown accustomed to. The gate is armed, but not with the normal electrical charge. No, I had only seen this a few times. It is charmed to not let anything or anyone in—or out, in this case—that doesn't have the access codes.

It takes a moment for the creature to realize she is locked inside the protective bubble with me. I sidestep her first flailing attempt, easily avoiding the edge of the weapon she holds and putting distance between Zane and me.

He reaches to grab the angel.

"Don't!" I warn.

He halts as if his life depends on it.

I am sure it did, but that little distraction cost me some blood. The angel's sword slices down my left shoulder with her second attack. The sting barely registers, but the oozing heat running down my arm does. Before she can get another blow in, I step closer, reaching for her wrist with as much speed as I can conjure.

I yank her forward, making it impossible for her to cut me again with her long sword. Her eyes widen, and I let a satisfied smile form. I relish her sudden terror as her ethereal soul slowly strips from her earthly form. It is glorious, but in some ways worse than Zane's father had been.

"I am so much more than any of you heavenly assholes ever thought. It will take an army to crush me," I snarl in her ear as I unsheathe Heaven's blade. I sink it right into the angel's stomach.

She sucks in her breath as her gaze drops to the knife I still grasp.

"Heaven's blade?"

"You bet your lily-white ass." I yank it out of her just as the last of her soul peels off her body.

Light radiates from where the blade pierced her, and she screams, throwing her head back with the force of it. I almost didn't catch the ding from my wrist announcing her death. Her body lifts off the ground and a millisecond later, she explodes in a wave of light that throws me into the air.

I land on the grass and the wind sucks out of me as if I am stuck in some weird vortex. I blink up at the brightening sky and try to take a full breath; I can't quite manage it. My ears ring as I push myself into a sitting position. The blade is still in my tightly fisted hand. I somehow am lucky enough that the ethereal blast hadn't sent me in Zane's direction. I sheathe it before I do any more damage and then look around. I am halfway across the yard.

The cars we were near had been pushed a few feet toward the house, and in some cases, into

117

each other. I scan the yard for Zane and my heart jumps into my throat when I can't locate him. I scramble to my feet and run toward the mass of metal.

In my mind, I scream for Nana, because in the pit of my stomach, I know something terrible has happened. But at least the Book of Fates hadn't rung its foreboding ding more than once, so he had to be alive.

The front door opens, and Nana runs out onto the front path like the world has gone up in flames. Her bare feet and nightgown tell me I woke her from sleep, abruptly. "What the..." She skids to a halt.

"Zane." I point at the cars. We both run toward the twisted mess. When I can't see his body above the crushed cars, I drop on my hands and knees, but the shadows play tricks on my eyes.

"Move!" Nana snaps, and I scramble out of the way. I'm breathing heavy, more from the panic than exertion.

The creak of metal sends a flurry of shivers through me and then one of the cars rights and slides to the side. Nana only has the power to heal. I glance up in time to see Papa's drapes fall back into place. She must have used her telepathic powers to call for his help and he moved the cars out of the way for her with his power of telekinesis. Light fills the space between cars, and I round the corner and stop in my tracks. My hand flies over my mouth at the sight before me.

Zane is still breathing, but barely. He was nearly crushed to death by the mass of metal that he had been thrown among. I sit down hard on the pavement. My throat tightens at the thought of losing him.

"Thank you," I squeak out.

"He's going to be out for a while." She wipes her face. "You don't look like you got through whatever that was unscathed." She nods toward my arm.

I glance down at the deep cut. I won't have the benefit of Nana's magic to heal it. "You have your medical bag here, right?"

"That needs stitches," she says as she comes closer.

"You can't touch me." I point at her. "But you can walk my father through patching me up." I glance around as Papa comes out of the house with flannel pants on.

"What happened?"

"An angel got through the charms you have up, and I used Heaven's blade." I climb to my feet and wave at the metal disaster surrounding us. The world tilts under my feet, and I reach out to the nearest car to get my balance.

"Can you help get Zane into the house and on the couch?" Nana asks Papa. "I'll go get your dad and get my bag." She nods toward the house. "Go sit at the kitchen table, please."

I weave my way inside and collapse on one of the wooden kitchen chairs, welcoming the dark room. I don't know what I am going to do. My plan didn't account for the bomb-like annihilation that happened when Heaven's blade was employed. I lean back and cover my face with my hand just before the overhead lights blink on.

Nana comes in, carrying her medical bag. She sets it on the table and puts on a pair of rubber gloves. I stare at her latex-clad hands and raise an eyebrow.

"Your father is on his way down to help, but I need to at least clean the wound before he stitches you up." She puts a package of fresh gauze on the table along with a bottle of iodine. "I want you to put your head down on the table and your arm out straight. This way, if you end up passing out, you will not fall. Okay?"

"But the blood."

She waves my words away and points to the table. I slide the chair so the arm rest is underneath the table and move my hair so it is as far away from my throbbing arm as possible and I lay that straight across the wood just like she instructed.

"That's perfect. Just don't move."

"What the Hell?" My father's voice echoes in the kitchen, making me jump a little.

Before I can speak, cool liquid douses my arm. The coolness transitions into a nasty burn, like fire had been poured in the cut, but I force myself to stay still. But that does not exclude the wailing curses that slip out of my mouth. I normally don't drop f-bombs, but right now, with the pain radiating from my arm and up my neck, I don't care whether I am grounded for a month for my inappropriate language.

"Take deep, slow breaths," Nana says. "I know it burns like holy hell, but I need to get the dirt out before your father stitches you up."

More burning sensations take hold and tears blur my vision. I don't even twitch this time, but man, my stomach becomes decidedly sour. I swallow the awful taste creeping up my throat and will myself into a state of relaxation. Focusing on the light reflecting in the middle of the large-screen television, I force myself to breathe in through my nose and breathe out through my mouth, like all those meditation videos I've seen recommend. I concentrate on each breath, counting the ins and outs, even when the prick of a needle pierces my skin and my vision blurs from tears.

You can do this, I tell myself. *Breathe.* I can almost hear Zane's calm tone saying the word in my head. God, I wish he was awake and in here so I could get lost in his green eyes and the sound of his voice.

If I could have, I would have leaned over and vomited on the floor, but I can't move. Not if I don't want my father to screw up what he is doing. Nana coaches him through each stitch. Her soft instructions are lost on me because I have to keep counting my breaths to keep my stomach in check through each pierce of the needle and tug of the sutures. My eyes and throat sting from the continuous flow of my tears.

Then comes another round of burning iodine, but by this time, the sting isn't as teeth clenching as the first two rounds.

After what seems like a lifetime, Nana says, "You can sit up now."

"I don't think I can," I say. "At least not without throwing up."

Something shuffles next to the chair.

"It's okay. There's a garbage can right next to you if you need it."

I push myself up and stare at the blood smearing the nice wood table. My stomach rolls, but settles down after a few deep breaths. By some miracle, I don't vomit. I lean back in the chair and close my eyes.

"Is Zane okay?"

"He's passed out on the couch in the living room," Nana says as a warm cloth wipes at my arm.

I looked up as my father attempts to clean the blood off my arm. His lips are set in grim determination. When his gaze meets mine, I see a flash of emotion. It isn't anger, either. I blink at him. He is supposed to be soulless, but that look tells me otherwise, like there is still a small piece of him hidden away underneath.

"You did amazing," he finally says. Then he crosses to the sink and rinses out the bloody cloth before returning and helping to clean up the table with Nana. The shuffling of feet upstairs makes me look up at the ceiling and then over at Nana as she tosses another soaked paper towel into the garbage.

"Everyone is here. We thought it best to hunker down in one place after what happened in New Hampshire." She keeps mopping up blood and spraying the disinfectant on the areas she has gotten clean.

My father drops to his knees to sop up the mess on the floor before the rest of the house comes in for breakfast. I bet there would not be a soul that could eat after taking one look at this mess.

"We were worried about you, though." Nana glances at my father as she continues to clean off the table. "Your dad filled us in a little."

"You have charms against angels?" I know they had charms against other things, but I didn't think they worked on heavenly beings.

She smiles. "When Lucifer is your sworn enemy, you invoke the most powerful magic that you can muster. My sister-in-law restored it to its former glory." She throws the last of the paper towels that are now soaked in only cleaner in the garbage can and packs up her medical bag before she grabs a soda and sits down across from me. She pushes the ginger ale across the tabletop. "I wanted to thank you for bringing them all back." She takes a heavy breath. "That really was quite a feat."

My father slides the chair out next to me and takes a seat. "It isn't without ramifications. Any time you cheat Death, there are consequences." He lets out a small laugh. "But damned if I know what they are, with Heaven throwing such a hissy fit over nothing."

I bite my lower lip. Why would Heaven risk short-circuiting the world? Granted, we humans had slid into the gutter recently, but that can't be it. If it is, why don't they just launch a meteor toward Earth and end it like that?

No. This feels more personal. More fearful, as if I am more powerful than Heaven. I blow out air. The angel that showed up here hadn't attempted to smite me. Instead, she attacked with a sword. "They can't smite me, can they?" I glance at my father.

He just shrugs. "I don't know what they can do to you. But I sure know what they can do to us. They've made that perfectly clear in that note of yours." He crosses his arms. "I, for one, am not going down without a fight."

Chapter 11

MOST OF THE DAY slips away as I sit in the chair across from the couch in the living room, just watching Zane sleep. My heart weighs heavy with how pale he still seems. Nana assures me he is healing, but he was in such awful shape when she got to him. Thankfully, I hadn't found him first. Otherwise, my freak-out would have been much more magnified.

The pocket door is closed, shutting off most of the noise from the back of the house, where everyone who had been at the cottage congregated. I wonder how many more I could have brought back before I collapsed from exhaustion if Faith hadn't closed the portal as quickly as she had.

If I had been thinking, I would have brought Zane's mom back, too. I close my eyes. She hadn't even crossed my mind. With a heavy sigh, I stand up slowly. Any fast moves make the world spin. Nana says that's from blood loss, but as long as I eat and drink, it should go away fairly soon. Which is good, because if I have to fight in this condition, the world will end in a matter of minutes.

I cross and sink to my knees as close to Zane as I dare.

"I'm sorry for being a bitch earlier."

Zane's eyes open, and he turns his head toward me before looking around the room. "What happened?"

"You nearly got crushed by a car."

He glances down at his body and then back at me. "Dr. Ryan?"

I nod and his head falls back on the pillow. "How bad?"

I don't answer, but all I can envision is his mangled body between the cars, with her healing light cascading over him like a faithful blanket.

128

"What happened?" he asks again and turns on his side, tucking his palms under his cheek as he faces me. His gaze lands on my arm and he sits up as though his memory just turned on full force. "You got hurt."

I let out a huff. It's nothing compared to what he's been through. He had been unconscious most of the day, healing under Nana's magic. "I have an ugly line of stitches under this gauze pad." I tap my arm gently, careful to avoid my injury.

He closes his eyes and creases develop in his forehead. It takes a moment for the memories to fully form, but when they do, his eyelids fly open, zeroing in on me. "The angel blew up."

"That pretty much sums up what happens with Heaven's blade." Faith and Alex had recounted their experience with the blade. My mother and father testified as well. In all cases, that is the result of sticking Heaven's blade into the flesh of an enemy. "It also makes me need to reconsider my grand plan of stealing their souls and stabbing them with Heaven's blade. That explosion would likely kill me, along with anyone in the vicinity."

He snorts at me, as if I am feeding him a line of pure bullshit.

"You don't believe me? Look at the cars in the driveway." I hook my thumb over my shoulder.

He rises slowly, testing out his legs as if he doesn't quite trust them. When he seems surer of himself, he crosses to the bay window. He stares at the car pile-up and lets out a slow, soft whistle. "It looks like someone plowed into all of them."

"Yeah. I bet you're glad you parked on the road."

He lets out a bark of a laugh as he glances back at me with a nod. "At least we have one undamaged vehicle if we need to make a quick getaway."

I snort a laugh, but as I think about this morning, my smile fades. "You were crushed in between that mangled mess."

He turns toward me with wide eyes.

"I told you. You were nearly crushed to death."

He glances down at his tattered and bloody clothing as if to make sense of it all. But his gaze keeps landing back on my bandage. "I caused that." He points at my arm.

I can't bring myself to lie and tell him he didn't cause me to get hurt. If he had backed off and let me handle it instead of trying to march in like a savior, I wouldn't have taken my eyes off the angel in attack mode. I meet his gaze and shrug.

"Maybe now you'll listen to me when I tell you I have to do this alone."

The look he gives me crushes that hope. He makes his way back to the couch and stretches out on it again, as if the effort to walk to the window has sucked what little energy he had from his muscles. I guess having another near-Death experience will do that. Hell, I am exhausted from the day's emotional and physical toll. My muscles throb with it. What I wouldn't give to stretch out beside him on the couch and snuggle.

"You look so sad," he says.

I nod. I am. All this is too much for me. At sixteen, I am not prepared for this much drama. "I'm completely disillusioned. Everything I believed about good and evil..." I glance down at my hands and shake my head. I don't want to voice the words flowing through my mind. Everything has turned upside down in my world.

"I know. And right now, I couldn't give two craps about forever." He puts his hand out for me to take it.

I stare at his sweet offering. What I wouldn't give to take his hands and fall into his arms. The number of emotional hits his gesture gives me nearly closes my lungs. My chin trembles and my eyes mist over in response, because as much as I want to, I can't. I blink and hot streaks slide down my cheeks.

"That's worse than escorting you to Hell myself." I move back in the chair, scraping it a few feet out of his reach in case he throws caution to the wind completely instead of letting me make the decision about his soul.

Heat continues tracing paths on my face, and I swipe at the tears, trying to regain my composure.

The air surrounding us shimmers, then fades, almost like a warning. Someone is in trouble.

Zane sits up, as if he can feel the disruption, too.

My gaze lands on the door and everyone else who is dear to me beyond it. My feet move before my brain registers, and I fling the pocket door open. Everyone is crowded against the far end of the family room, across from the sliding glass doors leading to the backyard.

The slider is open, and two reapers hold a bloodied Mandy in their grip. My father has his arms out for everyone to stay back. Even without a soul, his protective reflex is amazingly astute.

I filter through the room, mindful not to touch anyone.

"We tried," Mandy says when I get closer.

"Put her on the couch," I order. The other two reapers—one young enough to be my age, and the other probably in his fifties—bring Mandy to the couch and lay her down. Her left arm is torn through just above the elbow, leaving a jagged, dripping mess. Everything about her screams she is near drifting away. I turn with my heart pounding in my chest.

"Nana, please help her." I point at Mandy and make sure I extend my mental power to protect everyone in the room from the reaper's touch. The same protection that I shot out around Zane's father fans out over my family standing with wide eyes, observing this crazy scene.

"She can't," Mandy whispers.

"Yes. She can. I am protecting her and everyone else in this room from Death's touch." Just like my father before me, I protect those I care about from our deadly touch.

Nana steps forward and casts me a worried glance. "It won't grow back," she says, waving to the reaper's severed arm.

"I know. We'll find her a mechanical arm after all this if we need to, but if you don't help her, she's not going to make it."

"I don't know if my healing power will work on a reaper." Nana bites her lip and wrings her hands. She takes the final steps, but the closer she comes to Mandy, the paler she becomes.

"It's okay. The reapers can't hurt you. So, please just try," I say softly enough for her to hear.

Some of her color returns, and she leans down and presses a kiss to Mandy's forehead.

At first nothing happens, but then Nana's healing light blooms bright, nearly blinding us as it dances over Mandy's battered body. Mandy groans at first before she grits her teeth and stares wide-eyed as the unnatural jagged angles in her body straighten back into their natural state. The bruises in her already pale skin clear and even her severed arm heals up, as if someone repaired the raw end. At least her skin grows back, but Nana is right: the arm itself doesn't regenerate.

Mandy blinks and glances up at Nana and then at me with her mouth open.

I stifle a smile. I know how awe-inspiring Nana is and seeing it in the reaper's gaze makes me want to laugh. "What did you try to do?" I lower onto the edge of the coffee table now that she seems to be doing better.

"Malcolm, Jenny, and I tried to get Leviathan out of the cage they've got him locked in."

I glance at her arm, afraid to ask the question that pops into my head. "Did he do that?"

"No, the griffin standing guard did."

"Griffins exist?" I blurt the question and glance over my shoulder at my father.

"Beats the Hell out of me." He turns to Kylee, who stands near him. "Have you ever seen one?"

"No." Kylee glances at Phoebe and Smoke. "How about you?"

"Nope," both Smoke and Phoebe say in unison.

"There was one at Heaven's disposal," Papa's father says from the back corner of the room. "Nasty motherfucker, too."

Oh great. Leviathan is being guarded by another mythical beast. Just what I need. I wipe my face and turn toward the family still backed up into the wall area.

"You don't have to remain stuffed into the corner anymore. They won't hurt you. You all now have my protections against a reaper's touch." I glance around the room and my gaze lands on my father and his proud grin that is totally misplaced in the current situation.

"That's my girl."

I roll my eyes and grab one of the kitchen table chairs and pull it into the corner nearest the couch Mandy is on. The other two stand behind the overstuffed seat like sentries. I need to find out whether they have any other information about Heaven's impending attack.

None of the reapers seem eager to leave either. I'm not sure whether that's by design or whether they can't leave. After all, the protections on the house were pretty robust.

"How'd you get in?" I ask.

"You're our boss. We can get to you anytime, despite these rudimentary sigils." Mandy points to the piece of paper with the drawings Kylee had done to make everyone's whereabouts blind to the reapers.

"It protects the humans from us knowing where they are, though," the older reaper said. His grimace told me the sight of that sigil makes him as logy as it makes me feel.

Zane wanders over and takes a seat near me. I can tell he isn't exactly comfortable being near my emissaries. And he recognizes Mandy. He gives her a curt nod and sits as close to me as he can without touching me.

I scoot my chair into the wall, putting some distance between us. "Zane, you've met Mandy, but this is Jenny and Malcolm. Guys, this is Zane."

Zane sticks out his hand. "I'm Missy's boyfriend," he says, surprising the Hell out of me.

136

I stare at him like he had suddenly grown a second head. I am so conflicted where he is concerned, especially given our current no-touch circumstances, and I thought he was in the same mindset, but apparently not.

I guess my shock is on full display because Mandy asks, "Does she know that?" before she accepts his handshake.

He smiles and shrugs. "I don't know. But whether she likes it or not, I am not going anywhere."

"Must be nice to have such loyal subjects." Mandy gives me a raised eyebrow.

"They are not subjects." I don't like the way she refers to the people in this house. They aren't my subordinates. They are family—and some pretty powerful family members at that.

Mandy puts her hand out, splaying her fingers wide. "I meant no offense. It has been a very long time since I interacted in this realm."

I rein in my aggravation as Holly makes her way over to our growing circle. Although I am relieved to have the distraction, the closer people get, the more uncomfortable I become. I go to scoot my chair farther away, but the wall stops me. There is nowhere for me to go.

"Holly, this is Mandy, Malcolm, and Jenny. Guys, this is my best friend in all the world."

Holly gives handshakes all around. "I heard you say it's been a long time since you've been here. So, how long has it been?" Holly asks. Leave it to her to ask the questions no one else will voice after Mandy's awkward slip.

Mandy's mouth moves silently as she stares at the ceiling, counting on her only hand. "About sixteen hundred years. And that was just a brief visit." She glances around. "Things certainly have gotten advanced in the ways of comfort."

"What about you?" Holly asks Malcolm.

He shifts and puts his arm out to lean on the counter near me. When his hand brushes my arm, I gasp in horror. Light blooms from within him and flows into me in a rush that steals my breath just as efficiently as I've stolen his soul.

"No, no, no," I mutter, trying to stop the transfer. But I am helpless. If I lean too far away, I will connect with Zane, and my body will not allow that.

Malcolm's lips draw into a grimace and then he crumbles away like the reapers I destroyed at Thanksgiving. It isn't the same as a living being; they seem to be able to survive without a soul. But not a reaper. Without his soul, he is nothing but dust.

"No!" I cry just before his face disappears.

I can't stay inside. I can't deal with the shocked stares of everyone in the house, and I bolt out the back door, away from everyone. However, I can't outrun the truth of what just happened. My breath comes in distressed pants at the horror of an innocent mistake. With just a brush of skin, I destroyed that reaper.

"No!" I scream at the Heavens and fall to my knees as sobs rip from my chest.

A cold rain spritzes down over me, soaking my clothes and chilling me as I cry. No one comes out to collect me. Not even my father.

I can not do this. I can't live in a world where I am a monster. It's not in my makeup to be alone, never mind alone forever. My breath hitches again as the sobs turn to more like hyperventilating. I can almost hear Zane whispering "breathe" in my ear.

Just the thought of him both soothes the growing anguish and creates an emptiness in my soul. Tears mix with the rain as I take breath after breath like a fish gasping out of water. Somehow, oxygen finally flows into my veins, loosening my chest. My teeth chatter and as soon as I get my lungs under control, I glance over my shoulder at the house.

The door is closed and although my father leans against the glass watching me, he doesn't budge to try to console me. He's probably doing damage control inside. Everyone knows I'm dangerous to touch, but that little horrifying display certainly solidified the genuine threat.

I turn back toward the ocean when I spot Zane on the lounge chair, watching me. He gives me a half-hearted smile and pats the seat next to him. Damn him. He has such a wonderful heart.

Tears spring again and I blindly make my way to the chair next to him, mindful of where he is in relation to me.

"I didn't mean to..." I wave at the house and then collapse into the chair.

"I know. He barely brushed against you." He stares out at the ocean as if mesmerized by the sound of the rain and the waves. "It wasn't your fault."

"How long have you been out here?" The leather outfit I'm still wearing isn't as comfortable when it's wet, and I wish for a comfortable pair of dry jeans and a button-down shirt instead. The air around me swirls, and Zane's eyes widen.

My kick-ass boots remain, and they look just as good with jeans as the black duster. The sheath for Heaven's blade hangs comfortably on my hip from a stylish belt. And I don't really know why I chose white, especially considering it's raining, but the white button-up shirt seems to fit just right. Thankfully, we are both under the awning. Otherwise, my choice in color would be questionable at best.

"That seems like a handy power," he says, impressed.

"I'd forgo all these powers if I could get rid of this curse." As much as the willing of clothing and other items is fun and handy, I'd give it up in a heartbeat just to hug my family and kiss Zane.

142

Chapter 12

WHEN THE CHILL HAS my teeth chattering, we head back into the house and this time people give me a wide berth. It is enough to trigger a chuckle or two. Mandy and Jenny hadn't bugged out like I assumed. If I had been in their shoes, I wouldn't have stayed put. I would have been gone in a flash. They sat with the only witch in the group.

Raven Ryan leans over the coffee table, examining each of the items laid out across the wood.

I glance over Kylee's shoulder at the array of spices and crystals. "What are you doing?"

"After that disturbing display, your father was kind enough to explain what happened to you and why Heaven is in such an uproar." Raven glances up and meets my gaze. "And Kylee and I were going through some of these ancient magic tomes that Mandy retrieved for us. I think we may have found just the right spell to rid you of that curse," she says with a smile that only lasted a blink before it fades. "Unfortunately, there is an ingredient that is tricky."

"What's that?"

"The blood of a demon."

I straighten, and my stomach tightens at the thought. What the Hell would they need demon blood for? "How exactly does this spell work?"

"It's an ancient rite from the dawn of time. Or at least that's what I think, from some of the language. Of course, my decryption skills are rusty now that I'm back here, but in Heaven, I could decipher any language. With that said, it's risky. Especially if I translated it wrong. If even one stone is out of place or we miss an ingredient, it could backfire," Raven says, lulling me with her Irish accent.

"How so?" Zane says from a few feet away. Even he is giving me a wide enough berth to make my heart ache.

Raven huffs and glances at the paper with the entire translation written out in plain English, along with the laundry list of items. Most of the ingredients lay on the table, from crystals to pieces of wood and weeds to cinnamon and other spices that I know well enough from our kitchen, along with a handful of essential oils. It looks like a natural healing center instead of Papa's family room.

"It could capture her soul in the bloodstone." Raven meets my gaze.

I inhale and glance at my father, who doesn't seem the least bit fazed by her admission, so I turn to Tom Ryan, Raven's husband, and the one the angels originally sent here to destroy me. "How sure are you in her skills?"

He goes to speak, but Papa raises his hand, silencing him. "She saved Valerie from possession," Papa says. "I would not hesitate to put my life in her hands."

Raven glances over her shoulder and gives him a smile and a nod of thanks.

But it still leaves me itchy and uncomfortable. Sort of the same way Kylee and Michael had made me feel just before he tried to kill me.

"I'm still not sold on this," Zane says. "She is Tom's wife, right?"

"Mhm," Papa confirms.

I am sure he knows where Zane is going with his questioning. After all, Papa can dig into any mind he wants with no effort. But I am glad someone else besides me is having difficulty with this very convenient development. I hadn't even asked anyone for help with trying to find a mystical cure for my problem.

"Wasn't he sent to kill Missy?" Zane crosses his arms and glances at Kylee. "And didn't your husband actually try to kill her?" His sharp glare dances across them and lands on Mandy. "And you're a reaper. Weren't you part of the rebellion that caused all this shit to rain down on us?"

Holly cocks her head as she steps closer, inspecting those who had come up with this marvelous plan to get rid of my curse. "He has a point," she says, giving Zane's line of questioning a more solid ground. "What if the goal is to capture her soul and then destroy her?"

"Oh, child," Raven says softly, scanning the contents of the page. "Capturing her soul in the bloodstone won't doom us all."

Tom steps around in front of Raven, but she won't look at him. He sinks to his knee next to her. The crease between his eyes deepens and his lips turn into a deep frown of disappointment. "Really?" he says. "You're taking Heaven's side?"

She presses her lips together and stares at the ground.

Mandy looks between the two of them and then at me with wide eyes, as if she isn't in on the ruse.

"Do you know what that really means?" he asks.

Raven still avoids his gaze. "That we are all safe?"

Tom slowly shakes his head. "No. If she dies while she holds both roles, the world ends." He snaps his fingers. "Like that."

Raven finally looks up at him. "They said we'd all be safe."

Zane pulls the note that Mandy had given me out of his pocket and throws it on the table. "Does that sound like safe to you?"

Tom doesn't even spare the note a glance, but he does look at me. "I'm not willing to wipe out the world just because Heaven is afraid of a sixteen-year-old girl." He looks back at his wife. "No one here should be willing to do that. Hell, even the reaper looks sick at the thought." He waves at Mandy.

Raven glances at the dust-bound book in front of her and leans back on the couch, meeting my gaze. "They said you would destroy the world," she says to me.

"I don't plan on doing that. That seems to be Heaven's grand scheme."

She shakes her head, unable to grasp what we are telling her.

"Angels are dicks," Tom says. "You know that as well as I do."

I cross my arms and tilt my head. "How did they know I'd bring you back?"

She blinks. "They didn't. I was supposed to slip through in the event Tom failed." She glances at him. "And they promised we'd all be together again when this was over." She looks at the other side of the room where the kids were playing board games. "We were dead."

"And she brought us all back to life." He points at me. "That is God's power, not something made of evil. Heaven could have come and saved us from Lucifer. They could have saved all their blood, but they stayed up in the garden, saying that they couldn't fiddle with Fate. Well, Fate just interceded. And I'm placing my bets on her."

Kylee moves back on the couch, too. Her face is a mask I can't read. She shakes her head. "I thought you were genuine," she finally says in a tone that carries the same disgust I taste in the back of my throat.

She glances around at the people I brought back from the dead. "How many of you were coerced to do the same?" Kylee asks.

"I told them to go pound sand," Papa's father says. "I never trusted those bastards. They smile to your face and then rip you to shreds behind your back."

All of this talk is really grating on my nerves. If this is where people are trying to get to all their lives, it must be a horrible letdown. "I have a question," I say, capturing everyone's attention. "Is Heaven really that bad?" I look at Papa's father because it seems he has the most reservations of anyone in the room, even more so than Tom.

He tilts his head from side to side. "Heaven itself as a place isn't bad. It's quite peaceful, but the angels that run it remind me too much of my sadistic older brother to really buy into it all. They don't like free thought." He shrugs. "That's the best way I can describe them. They want people who kiss their ass and believe they are the perfect creations. They aren't. They are just as flawed as we are, but they are blind to that. And anyone or anything that is stronger than they are, they fear."

"They do things that conflict with what they are supposed to represent," Tom says. "And with all the archangels graceless, it makes it difficult to restore any semblance of order. Even they are pretty much shit on at this point."

I blink at that. Archangels shit on? That just did not compute at all. "It seems they are sending the people closest to Papa, or to Alex and Faith, to do their dirty work, but I'm not sure there is anyone else at their disposal to send, based on all of you." I wave my hand toward the people who I pulled out of Heaven and breathed life into. "They've locked Levi away in Purgatory somewhere, and they are planning on attacking us all in the next twenty-four hours." I scan the room, making eye contact with the thirty or so people, including the kids, who were present. "You know how I came to be this..." I hold up my hands and slowly fist them before I let them drop by my side again. "This cursed thing. So, what would you do if you were me?"

Raven sighs and pulls the book back in front of her.

"What are you doing?" Holly asks.

"Instead of crafting a way to bind her, I need to see if there is anything in this book to free her of her curse." She pushes all the contents of the table into the corner and flips open the book.

"Thank you, but that doesn't address the angels."

"No, but it will give them one less reason to want to destroy you." She meets my gaze and then looks at the space surrounding me the same way Tom had.

Tom leans back on his heels. "You can see her aura?"

She nods and glances at her hands. "I just didn't want to believe what I was seeing."

"It's the reason I immediately discounted Heaven's orders."

"What's wrong with my aura?"

"Not a damn thing," Tom answers. "It's actually the most stunningly pure aura I've ever seen, and that includes CJ's." He points at Papa. "Sorry bro, but hers is brighter and it looks like it's infused with rainbows. There is a total absence of darkness, like I'd expect from being Death." He shrugs. "Not even the angels in Heaven have auras like that. I just wish I had met her before she took those positions to see if it was the same."

"It's always been like that," Faith says from the kitchen table. She smiles at me. "The only time it seemed to dull at all was after her parents visited and she dipped into her separation depression."

I shift my feet and glance over my shoulder at Zane. This conversation isn't helping me. I clear my throat. "That's all well and good, but I need to talk battle strategy while we all still have our wits about us."

"Are you really going to trust them?" Zane asks, scanning the room with a skeptical eye.

"I have no choice. Everyone knows the stakes. And if they cross me, there will be some sort of reckoning that won't make anyone happy."

I glance at Mandy and then Raven, Kylee, and Michael to make my point. I wonder whether I had the ability to test alliances like I had with the reapers. I close my eyes and send the same power I'd used to ferret out traitors in the reaper federation across the house like a bomb plowing over the wicked.

I open my eyes. Jenny, the other reaper, gasps as her fingers turn to dust and the ash gray spreads until all that is left is a human form of ash before it explodes outward and disappears before it covers everything in the room.

"What did you just do?" Mandy asks with her eyebrows riding high on her forehead. The rest of the room mirrors her.

"Sorry, but I had to be sure. I did the same mental sweep of the room that I did in Kittery with the federation," I say, a little rattled that even one being is toasted by my protection sweep. I don't know what I would have done had one of the living people in the room dropped dead, but I needed the comfort of knowing that when I turn my back, I wouldn't find a butcher knife embedded between my shoulder blades.

Chapter 13

FEEDING NEARLY THIRTY PEOPLE seems to be a challenging thought. Challenging enough for Papa to order pizza and wings instead of trying to figure out what they have in the way of food in their pantry. It'll take a while for them to arrive and the newly living use the time to catch up with those around here.

The doorbell rings and all talk halts. There's no way the pizza place made ten pies and delivered them in less than ten minutes.

"Relax. It's April. I thought she might want to see her father." Papa meets Tom's gaze before he leaves the room.

A moment later, April steps into the kitchen. Her normally manicured hair looks like she ran over from their house across town. She is breathing hard too, so maybe she did. When her gaze lands on her father, her hand flies to her mouth. Tears spring from the corner of her eyes and then her gaze shoots around the room until it lands on me.

"You?" she asks.

Although Heaven had originally sent him, I brought him back to life, so I take the credit with a nod.

One minute, she's standing still and the next, she's in a full-out run, closing the distance between her and her father. She jumps the last couple of feet and throws her arms around her father's neck, nearly knocking him back into the wall. Her shaking sobs fill the room. Even though she's seen him in Paradise Cove over the years, I guess having him there in the flesh is different.

My throat tightens because I know just how she feels. Every time I saw my parents, that rush of gratefulness is overwhelming. I glance at my parents watching from across the room with wine glasses in their hands. That warm rush fills my veins and I blink back tears.

It is nice to see the good that I had done by bringing them back to life.

As I scan the room, families form cliques. The elder Ryans and Williamses hang together near the front window. All the Andreas clan stand in their little circle except for Kylee. She is talking with my folks and Phoebe and Smoke on the other side of the kitchen island, almost as if they are all removed from the dynamics of the family reunion going on.

Nana and Papa follow April and stand with their brother and his family, along with Alex and Faith.

That leaves us, my little clan of Zane, Holly, and Mandy, by the sliders to the backyard and the younger kids between the Andreases and the elder Ryans.

The dynamic in the room is odd and, despite the multitude of conversations going on, a stressful undercurrent still thrives in the air.

I know I'm stressed just by the dull ache from having my muscles clenched for so long. Even my jaw hurts. But hunger partly fuels my tension. Despite Nana's continued offerings of food, I hadn't eaten much today. My stomach just doesn't want any part of food. At least I drank enough juice and soda during the day to feel like myself again. Well, all except my arm. That just throbs with an underlying itch. It'll drive me mad if I don't have anything to keep my mind occupied.

My lack of appetite changes the moment the pizza arrives. The scent of Italian spices and tomato sauce makes my mouth water. Zane seems to have the same reaction, too. He licks his lips as the tops are thrown back from the pizza boxes on the island in the kitchen and the counter. Once my plate is piled high with Hawaiian pizza, I find my way back to my seat in the corner, thankful that no one has claimed the chair.

I don't care that it's the second night of pizza. I could eat this every day of the year if given the chance, but Alex and Faith limited our pizza runs to once a month. They wanted us healthy, with a rounded palate. Whatever the Hell that means.

The only thing that would make this the perfect meal would be a tray of Goldenrods fudge. I love good, rich chocolate fudge, and Goldenrods has the best. I wish we had one of the fudge trays they display in their picture windows to entice the public to come into the store. I can almost smell it and damned if that would make this horrific situation flow a little smoother.

The air over the counter shimmers and within a blink, an industrial-size tray of fudge appears.

I let out a soft laugh and meet Zane's gaze. He smiles. It seems like the first genuine smile to grace his lips since he saw me in the school hallway with Levi. It reaches his eyes, making them sparkle.

We reach for the sweets at the same time and both stop. He waves for me to go ahead and I know as a guest in the house, he should go first, but I am craving the decadent dessert. I grab a corner and tear off a piece. It isn't cut, so a fair-size chunk comes off and I grin at his dropped jaw. Although I could devour the enormous piece in my hand, I break the piece in half and put the smaller part back in the pan for him.

He does not hesitate. He scoops up the fudge and nearly shoves the entire piece in his mouth. I'm not much more civil about it. After all, it is Goldenrods fudge, which is on par with their salt-water taffy. Knowing he is just as crazy for their fudge makes my heart carve another notch on the "do not let go of him" pole, regardless of our hopeless situation.

"I could eat this whole pan," he whispers low enough for only me to hear.

"You'd have to fight me for it."

Thunder cracks outdoors and we both jump. Our gazes swivel toward the glass sliding doors. Darker clouds roll in at an unnatural pace, blocking out the late afternoon sun that had temporarily broken through. It's something you would see in a horror movie. Lightning dances on the water in a deadly march straight toward the bluff where Papa's house sits.

Papa steps to the window and closes his eyes. He dips his head and the surrounding air electrifies.

His power tastes like the sweetest cotton candy, and I swallow my last bite of fudge to drown out just how insignificant I feel next to Papa. His power could split the world in two, and yet Heaven never once tried to kill him because of it. Maybe that's because he's angelic in nature, but his magic could be just as deadly as my touch.

"Don't you already have the property protected?"

"It only goes in a complete circle around the house. The far end of the yard near the rock wall isn't covered. Besides, a little stronger incentive to keep them away never hurts." He smiles down at me and I can't disagree.

A single angel lands just inside the rock wall near where the protection charms on Papa's property end. Papa reaches for the door, but my father stops him.

"I got this. Just don't toast me in the process." He steps outside. He puts his hand out and gives me a curt shake of his head when I slip from my chair to join him, and then he closes the door behind him.

He crosses to the edge of the pool on this side. The angel comes closer but stops after a few steps as his eyes widen and he looks beyond my father, right at Papa. Even I can see the fury building in the intruder just by how red his face gets. His gaze snaps back to my father. My father had to have warned him in some way, but I couldn't be sure.

"What are they saying?" I ask. The rest of the people in the house gather around as well, upping my unease.

"I don't know. I can't read your father's mind and I can't read the angel, but from his stance, he's not happy with whatever your father is saying," Papa said.

Thunder rumbles in response, rattling the windows.

I move back into my corner, careful not to bump into anyone. I reach for another piece of fudge. A hand grabs my wrist and I gasp, snapping my gaze to the one stupid enough to touch me. Gabriel's eyes are wide and I'm sure mine are the same.

Zane goes to grab Gabriel.

"Don't touch him!" I can't help the panic in my voice, but at least Zane heeds my warning.

161

Light flares around us and I breathe him in. Purity and Old Spice. That's what he smells like and his soul—despite the horrific trials that he suffered and died from—fills me with calmness, followed by a hollowed-out feeling that I'd ruined yet another person with this curse. The brightness that had surrounded him before fades and he looks at the connection of his hand around my wrist.

"I just cut that piece," he says in a deadpan voice.

My eyes follow where I was reaching. A kitchen knife lays next to a neatly cut square. Gabriel lost his soul over a piece of Goldenrods fudge.

How asinine is that?

"Oh." That's all I can muster. "I'm sorry," I add as an afterthought. My heart aches for him and he lets go of my wrist, scoops up the chocolate and wanders away as if nothing happened.

I know better. Everyone in the room staring at me knows better, too.

I turn toward Zane, feeling that welling panic attack coming on.

The slider door opens, and my father steps inside, closing the glass behind him.

162

"What the Hell just happened?" my father asks.

"I was reaching for a piece of fudge without looking and Gabriel grabbed my wrist."

My father looks beyond me. "Goldenrods?" He points, as if the fudge had made him forget his question.

"Of course. Where else would I conjure a tray from?" I roll my eyes. "But that's beside the point," I add as he crosses and cuts himself a piece, too.

"Well, if you're going to lose your soul over something, this fudge isn't a bad thing to have it happen over." He plops it into his mouth and smiles.

"What happened outside?" Papa asks with a tone as impatient as I feel.

My father doesn't answer right away. He closes his eyes and puts up his finger, announcing silently that he'd be with us in a moment. "You want a piece, hon?" he asks my mother around a mouthful of the confection.

"Dad," I snap. Everyone is focused on him and waiting to hear our Fate since it's no longer written in my handy-dandy Book of Fates.

"I bought us another twenty-four hours before all of Heaven's angels descend and smite us to Hell." He cuts another piece and holds it in his outstretched hand for my mother.

She rolls her eyes and crosses to him, plucking the fudge out of his hand. I can almost hear her "Oh my God, really?" but she doesn't speak. Instead, she nibbles on the fudge. If we had been in any other situation, she would have gobbled it up as fast as either Zane or I had before the angel came.

"Minus the archangels. They did not want any part of this," he adds after he swallows a second piece. "However, after that light show in here, I'm not so sure they'll abide by the terms. I think that angel recognized the transfer of a soul."

"What do you mean, transfer of a soul?" Gabriel asks as he finishes licking his fingers.

"Wait. They are going to kill us?" Jessica Ryan, Papa's mother, asks from the far side of the room.

"That's their current threat. But the fact that angel was afraid of CJ's barrier, I'm not so concerned. Now, if something were to happen to him, well, then we'd have to have another conversation." My father reaches for another piece of fudge.

I slap his hand and shake my head. "I'm sure others will want some of that," I say when he tilts his head like a damn puppy.

The creases on his forehead smoothed out. "Sorry."

"You all need to get some rest if we have a prayer of figuring this out." Papa looks pointedly at me, as if he knows just how exhausting all this is. Although Gabriel's soul had given me a boost of energy, unlike the reaper earlier.

He crosses to me. "I think you should stay in the panic room with your family," Papa says softly. "It has almost every kind of warding and protection known to man."

"What if they come for us while I'm sleeping?"

His lips twitch into a secret grin. "They can't get in. And if they get through the protections we have in place, they'll have to deal with me." He shakes the smile off his face and meets my gaze. "You need sleep." He nods toward the stairwell. "Alex knows the code. The couches pull out and there are already linens down there." He turns to Zane. "See that she actually gets some rest."

Zane nods, but we all know that if I decide to get up and leave, there is no possibility of physically stopping me without someone else losing their soul.

165

Chapter 14

THE ROOM IS PITCH black. I lie on the pull-out closest to the door. Zane's on the other bed. I am shocked that Alex and Faith let us come in here alone, but they, along with my mother, insisted that I get rest.

"You're still awake," Zane says from the other bed.

"Yes."

"Why?"

I sigh. "Because I can't stop thinking about that binding spell. If my soul was captured in the bloodstone…"

"No. Just no. If you become soulless, you won't have any inclination to save us, and I think you'd be very dangerous without a soul." He sounds annoyed. "Besides, if you won't entertain me losing my soul, why the Hell should I contemplate you losing yours?"

"Didn't anyone ever tell you life isn't fair?"

The springs of his bed squeak, and I hold my breath. But hands scraping against the wall searching for a light switch fills the dark just before all the lights blaze on, blinding me. Zane glares at me.

He crosses to the end of my bed where all that separates us is sheets and a comforter. "That was pretty shitty." He climbs on the end of the bed, crawling with his legs on the outside of mine, the same with his arms.

"What are you doing?" I pull the blankets up to my chin as the weight of him pins me under the sheets. My breathing labors and I will him to stop moving. I will him not to touch me, even though every cell screams for him.

He stops moving, frozen by my wish, and his jaw tightens as his glare pierces through me. "Let me go."

I shake my head slowly. "No."

"How can I love someone and hate them at the same moment?" His green eyes nearly glow with malice and underneath a caring so strong that I nearly falter.

"You hate me?"

He closes his eyes, still stuck mid-crawl. "I'm angry," he finally says. "I want to slam you against a wall and then kiss you into oblivion. If we are going to all die tomorrow, I at least want a damn kiss."

"I can give you fudge," I say softly and try on a smile.

His eyebrows rise as if he's considering the alternative. "As much as I like candy, it's not the same."

"Please go back to your bed," I plead, allowing him to back up if he chooses. But if he uses the sudden release of my mental hold as a sign of weakness and starts forward again, I'll make him go to his own bed. If I think he's mad now, *that* would make him furious.

"Fine," he says after a few minutes of a staring showdown between the two of us. He crawls off the bed and stomps to the light switch, slams it off, and stomps across the room. Flesh connects with metal in a subtle bang, followed by him cursing under his breath, "Goddamn it!"

"You okay?"

"Yeah," he groans. "I didn't need that little toe on my left foot."

"Ouch."

"No kidding. These bedframes are fucking dangerous in the dark."

"Yeah, well, you could have just left the light on, you know."

"You won't sleep if the light is on."

Damn, he actually knows me better than I gave him credit for. I would have totally just stared at the ceiling until someone came and got us out of the room. Still, I might just have that issue in the dark, too.

I don't answer him either. He knows he is right. I don't need to confirm it, and if I denied it, he would know I was lying. Besides, I don't want the awful taste lies leave in my mouth, so I say nothing.

Silence fills the absolute blackness surrounding us. I can't see my hand in front of my face, never mind the ceiling.

"I'm sorry," I whisper.

"For what?" he says, as if I had just pulled him from the edge of sleep.

"For bringing Levi to school."

The quiet stretches out between us as the wedge I just shoved in place pushes us apart.

"So, you'd rather have me dead?" There is a bite to his words.

"No. I..." What can I say to erase his aggravation? "I just wish you had never..." I close my eyes and growl in frustration. Anything I say right now will be wrong, and I certainly don't want to wish us back in time to change things, because that would mean that Zane Bradley died on Thanksgiving. "I wish I could lie in your arms and sleep."

"You can."

"No. I can't without harming you worse than your father ever did. Don't you see? Your soul is everything I love about you. Destroying that destroys you." My voice rasps out of my throat as I try to regain my composure, but I can't get hold of my emotions, so I lay them bare for him to see. "I can't voluntarily give you either the book or the scythe just to see if it will work, knowing you will die either way. I can't kill you. I can't strip you of your soul, and worst of all, I can't touch you."

"I can't let the angels slaughter you. *I* can't watch that."

"How do you know that's how it will end?" Irritation flares up. Hadn't he seen what I was capable of on a small scale at Thanksgiving when I annihilated the reapers who wanted to cause us all harm?

"Because everything good in my life is eventually crushed to dust."

That is a conversation killer, and it wipes the mounting frustration right from my bones. It isn't his lack of faith in my abilities, and that makes me feel better and worse at the same time. The circumstances of his life differ vastly from mine and if I, for a moment, were to put myself in his shoes, I would cling to whatever this insanity is between us, too.

"I'm not going to die."

"Can you guarantee that, or is that just to appease my insecurities?" The growl is back in his voice.

"Why do you think the angels are so afraid of me?" I ask, trying like hell to avoid making a promise I myself am not sure about. I have no intention of dying, but then again, the best laid plans always seem to go awry.

"Changing the subject?"

I let out a soft laugh. "Trying to, yes. I keep coming back to why would the angels want to destroy me. And the only thing I can think of is they are afraid. But I don't know why, and I feel that is the key to all this."

"It's simple. They know you are a force, and a wild card at that. You've done things no one else ever has. At least that's what your father said when we went to the pizza place." He sighs heavily. "You are the unknown."

"Levi once called me an enigma." I curl up on my side, facing the direction he is in. "I miss that monster. At least with him near, I felt like I had a fighting chance."

"I wonder how they caged him. That seems odd."

"Do you think the griffin is as big as Levi in his natural form?" Worry etches its way under my skin. I hadn't given much thought to how they got Levi under control. "And do you think their attempting to smite him actually hurt him?" My chest constricts. "And then the griffin attacked him?"

"Stop." Zane's voice holds authority. "Don't speculate. That will drive you bonkers."

"Bonkers?"

His chuckle warms me. "Better than batshit crazy."

"It is, I guess. Right now, everything seems a little more batshit crazy than it has all year, and that's certainly saying something."

"Agreed. I need some sleep."

"You slept most of the day."

"Being unconscious and sleeping aren't the same and you know it. You're the one with a visible wound. Get some shut-eye. That's an order. Or I'll just come over there and bother you again."

"Fine." Instead of staring at nothing, I close my eyes and start counting my breaths. Somewhere around the two hundred mark, I drift off in earnest.

Chapter 15

BLINDING LIGHT FILLS THE room, and for a moment, I think the angels are attacking. I sit up and raise my hand, squinting.

Holly's giggle breaks through the cobwebs in my head and her red hair forms beyond my hand as she comes closer to the bed.

"What time is it?" I glance over at the fold-out couch next to me where Zane had been. It is no longer out. The couch has been put back together and the sheets and comforter are folded up neatly on one side. I glance at where the bathroom is, expecting the door to be closed, but it's wide open.

"Where's Zane?" I look back at Holly.

"He got up a few hours ago and said to let you rest. But damn, girl. It's almost two in the afternoon."

My heart skips in my chest. I nearly slept the day away. And it could be my last damn day. "Why didn't anyone wake me earlier than this?" I jump out of bed and don't wait for her to answer. Instead, I bolt for the bathroom because I don't want to end up soiling the floor.

Holly follows to the door and waits until I throw it open after doing my business and splashing water on my face. I open the door to her standing near enough to give me a start.

She continues the conversation. "Because you needed the rest, and they used the time to figure out a way to break your curse."

I hurry by her, and then stop and spin around. She's still leaning on the wall. But the grin on her face causes my pulse to pick up. Hope shines down on me. "Did they?"

She nods. "At least they think they did."

My entire form jolts with the news and I don't wait for more information. I bolt upstairs and

176

almost plow over Smoke as I round the corner. Thankfully, I am able to pivot enough to not brush into him. I stop in my tracks at the array of spices, crystals, oils, and patterns pasted to the walls. The house smells like burned rosemary, and smoke still lingers in the air.

"You found a way?" I ask, out of breath, to no one in particular.

"We think so. It's not tested, but I think it will work," Raven says, studying the book on the counter.

A chair sits in the center of a pentagram within a circle they had drawn on the floor. There are more crystals at points along the circumference. Under the chair sits a smooth oblong beach pebble in a shallow grinding bowl.

Distrust blooms and I meet Zane's gaze from across the room. "What do you think?" I need to know his gut feeling about all this. As excited as Holly was downstairs, I can't help but let hope bloom, especially considering she was the first to truly question their intentions beyond Zane.

He lifts one shoulder. "I don't know enough about it to comment, but they seem sincere this time."

I meet Raven's gaze and she doesn't look away, unlike her earlier bid that included demon blood in the equation. "What are the risks?"

"You might get a stomachache from the drink. It's not all that pleasant." She pushes a cup across the counter and hooks her thumb toward the couch. "Your mother tried it to be sure it wouldn't harm you."

My mother waves from the couch and sends a half smile as she feeds some round disks into her mouth.

Raven taps the opened canister of Tums. "You'll probably need a few of these when it's done, too."

I lean over and take a whiff of the concoction. It smells like Papa's bourbon gone bad, mixed with twenty-week-old vegetables that had browned in the vegetable bin. My throat closes and I step back. "What's in it?"

"Kale."

That explains the bad vegetable smell.

"Dandelion greens, peppermint, cayenne pepper, lemon juice, and brandy, mixed with the blood of angels and ancients alike."

No wonder I want to vomit at the smell. I glance at my mother again. "How long ago did she take it?"

Raven glances at the clock on the stove. "A couple of hours ago. She's not as green as she was before."

"How much time is there before the angels come?" I ask my father. My heart has already made the choice for me. I am doing this if my time hasn't already run out.

"You have about five hours. Do you want to try this now or after you kick their asses back to Heaven?" he asks.

The way Zane looks at me is enough to decide. If there is any possibility of granting his wish, I am taking it. "Now." I grimace at the cup and then meet Raven's gaze. "What do I need to do?"

"Drink that and keep it down. And then sit in the chair and we'll do the rest."

I pinch my nose and pick up the cup. Without overthinking it, I tip it into my mouth, swallowing until it is all gone. The nose pinching helped, but I still shiver and gag my way to the chair. I concentrate on one of the sigils taped to the wall, willing my stomach to accept the drink.

My eyes burn from it. So does my throat. My stomach makes a roaring growl as it begrudgingly keeps the liquid in check.

I don't dare look away from that drawing because if I do, I will hurl. Zane steps in front of the picture and for a moment I think I'm going to lose it all over the floor, but the hope in his green eyes gives me the courage to swallow the vileness in my throat and keep that drink down.

"Breathe," he whispers and then others join him, clasping hands as they line the outer edges of the circle drawn on the floor.

From behind me, Raven chants words in a language I've never heard. The rest join in, including Zane. I watch in fascination as the words form tendrils of smoke, each one drifting toward me. The more times they chant, the more tendrils join the fray inside my circle.

I still keep Zane's gaze, ignoring the gathering smoke. Until miniature lightning bolts rain down around me. His eyes widen, but he keeps on saying the incantation, increasing the smoke and the clouds building above me.

I grip the arms of the chair. My heart races in my chest, making me forget about my sour stomach. I jump with every strike of light and so does Zane.

They all keep going, as if the energy being created in the circle is also fueling them. It is strange and scary and exhilarating. Rumbling starts above me. Then a blinding light encompasses me. I think I yelp, but I can't be sure.

All I know at this moment is absolute weightlessness, and then I crash down in the chair with enough force to rattle my teeth.

Zane looks a little pale, and he's pressed to the wall. I glance around at the rest of the group. Holly's hair looks as if she's been standing near the rock wall in the backyard during a nor'easter windstorm. My mother stands next to Holly with the same windblown features, but at least she doesn't look green anymore. My father stands on the other side of Zane with a grin, like whatever happened entertained him.

Alex, Faith, Nana, and Papa, although windblown, didn't look as rattled as Zane and Holly looked. Behind me, Raven, Tom, and Papa's parents fill in the circle.

"What happened?"

Zane remains speechless.

"Did it work?" I ask when no one speaks.

"There's only one way to find out," my father says. "Who wants to be the guinea pig?"

Zane went to move.

"No." I point at him. "You just stay right there." I turn around and look at Raven. "Since this was your thing..."

She pales and glances at Tom.

"Oh, for Heaven's sake." Kylee pushes through, breaking the neat little circle surrounding me, and grabs my wrist.

181

Light flares around us and her soul yanks from her body so fast, I don't even feel the transition. One minute, it was just me, and the next, Kylee's essence surrounds me before absorbing like the fading froth in a cooling bubble bath.

She stares at me and blinks. Her eyes widen for a moment and she lets out a soft laugh. "I wasn't Heaven bound, anyway." She winks at me.

"She's not wrong, you know," my father says.

"Did she just..." Michael points as Kylee heads back in his direction.

"No one was moving, so I took on the role of test subject. I really have nothing to lose. Well, I could have died if she didn't have that save-the-people-here spell going on all of us."

"But your soul?" Michael says.

"I'm not going to Heaven, Michael."

He glances at his father. "But he was a vampire for centuries and was still in Heaven."

"I'm not like your father. He is the archangel Gabriel's son, and before that he was human. I'm not."

His eyebrows arch as if this just doesn't compute.

"I'm not immortal anymore, but I wouldn't say I'm human."

"Technically, I think you became human once your siren was removed," my mother says. "But I don't think you could end up within the pearly gates."

"See? So just accept that I'll be a little less subtle and we'll continue raising our kids and hunting things like we normally do for as long as we are here. Of course, that could end this evening, but let's cross our fingers that Missy doesn't get snuffed out by those winged bastards." She smiles.

Disappointment flows in like the tide. Sneaky thing, too. One minute, I am fine and the next, my stomach decides that the crap I drank needs to be forcefully evicted. I make it to the kitchen sink without vomiting on anyone or touching them before the liquid escapes my tightly clamped lips.

I turn on the water as I heave, trying to clean the vile splatter from the spotless stainless steel. Someone pulls my hair away and rubs my back softly. When I finally spit out the last of the gross stuff, I take a mouthful of water from the faucet, swish it around my mouth, spit and then look at who was helping me.

Kylee gives me a soft smile. "It's the least I can do, considering I had been part of a plot to kill you and fulfill Heaven's asinine plans." She hands me a paper towel.

I wipe my mouth and shut off the water. "Sorry," I whisper, unsure of what I am apologizing for. She took the chance by stepping in and touching me when she wasn't sure whether it would strip her soul.

As far as my sins are concerned, my list is growing, and I don't even know where to start to atone.

Chapter 16

I TAKE A SEAT in the corner near Papa's sound studio entrance and stare out at the ocean. The world has just a few hours left before its possible demise and my entire mood sours with the thought. I can't seem to figure out my next move, except to fight.

The group has exhausted the options left to us. We even discuss trying that first spell to trap my soul in the bloodstone. But Zane won't have that. To be honest, no one is really for that, considering the price for failing.

"What if Missy were to give up both roles to two others?"

"I'm not killing anyone in this room to save myself," I snap and glare at him. "I'm not planning on losing, so you all can stop this little exercise in futility."

"I've already told you I can take on one of the roles." Zane crosses his arms. "Wouldn't that call off this insane battle?"

"You will stop breathing. What the Hell do I have to do to get that into your thick skull? Besides, we all saw the failed attempt to give the role back to my dad." I wave at my father. "I'm not trying something on you or anyone in this room, only to have you die and still be in this situation."

"She has a point," my father mutters, staring out at the ocean.

"He doesn't have a soul. Don't you think that might have something to do with why it failed?"

"I'm not betting your life on something so thin." Truth be told, that is the reason I initially thought the scythe wouldn't bond with him like it had with me, but I am not about to admit that to Zane. Not when so much is at stake.

"Everyone's life is already on the line."

An alarm buzzes and my father looks at his watch and then at me as those weird thunder clouds form again. But this time, they are gathering faster and more violently than before. Instead of retreating, I open the door.

"Make sure no one comes out," I say to my father and then close the door behind me. I cross far enough away to keep those in the house safe and stand on the lawn, using the pool as a buffer. If I can use that mass of water to my advantage, I will.

I close my eyes and wish for the leather battle gear I wore for the reaper standoff instead of the jeans and button-up I still have on.

The wind swirls around me as my outfit morphs into what I want. My scythe and Book of Fates also grow to their normal size, as I will them. I face the ocean, waiting.

A throat clears behind me, and I turn to Zane standing within a few steps from me. I glance at the door and my father is sitting on the ground, rubbing his jaw with the door still open.

"Did you hit my father?" I swing my sharp gaze to Zane's.

Zane glares at me as I hold both the Book of Fates and Death's scythe, waiting for Heaven's promised onslaught. I'm sure I look like a deity. At least, that is what I am trying to project. And he knows I am prepared to battle all of Heaven to keep my station and not put anyone I care about in harm's way.

He knows I don't want anyone saddled with the burden of forever, either.

Yet he still has his hand out, expecting me to concede. He is in. He is willing to sacrifice his entire future to keep me safe. He is too much like me in that respect. But for him, it is only about keeping me safe. For me, it's my entire family. Hell, the entire world—because the last time Heaven's wrath took out the single entity, the big bang happened.

If they kill me, who knows what will happen. It could be such a cosmic blowout that all of Earth is doomed.

Zane has no powers. He has no hope of commanding armies. Zane's lips thin as he glances behind me, shifting my attention. I turn to look over my shoulder and the scythe is yanked from my grip.

My gasp fills my world, and everything turns into slow motion as I pivot back to Zane, meeting his wide, terrified gaze.

Zane has the scythe in a two-fisted grip, owning it. He took it from me with the same intent I had taken it from my father on the day after Thanksgiving. He wants the job. Breathing be damned.

A ding sounds from my Book of Fates.

I can't look at it.

I can't breathe.

I can't take it back from him. If I inadvertently touch him, I'll siphon his soul. Making this all so much worse.

"Why did you do that?" I scream over the roar of the cyclone that overtakes us.

He sends a shaky smile and shrugs. "The world is better with you in it."

Oh, how I want to rip it from his grasp, but deep down I know, either way, Zane is dead. My book says so, and this time, I have no control over the outcome. I lower the electronic pad, which has his name blaring on the screen like a silent siren of doom, and wish the book into a charm before I drop it. The book shrinks and attaches to my charm bracelet like it always does at my command.

No sooner have I taken care of the Book of Fates than the essence of Death peels from every cell, dropping me to my knees in sheer agony. Being drawn and quartered would have been less painful, but I remain lucid as every stabbing pain wracks my body. Death's essence intertwines around Zane—looping, testing, surrounding him—before it gathers between us, still pulling the last tentacles from within me.

Then it shoots into Zane's chest in a mass of blinding light.

Zane bows backward with the force of it. His arms flail to his sides as his body lifts from the ground. He looks like Christ on the cross with his arms wide out and his head tilted back. A silent scream of anguish frames his face. I have no idea how he holds onto the scythe, especially with his eyes rolled back in his head so far, but he grips the rod with the whitest knuckles I have ever seen, almost as if he knows how important it is to keep a grip on that magical rod.

After the last of Death's essence rips from my cells, small orbs free from me. One circles around me as if it recognizes me, and then shoots out of the vortex encircling us. I have no idea what they are, but the release of that light makes me feel freer than I have felt since my parents showed up at Alex's house a little over a week ago, like I finally woke from a horrible nightmare.

Zane lowers to the ground with the scythe still in his grip and then his arm falls across his body, pinning the weapon to his chest, and the light surrounding us fades. The house comes into view and I scan the yard behind me.

I now know why Zane had taken the scythe from me. My eyes widen at the legion of angels just outside the marred crop-like circle that Zane and I are in, frozen as if the events of the past couple of minutes had them unsure of their task of ridding the Earth of a duel-deity.

I pray Zane's death won't leave me in their crosshairs. If it does, this isn't about holding both roles in perpetual fortitude. This is just a power play. If that's the case, I am more than willing to yank every soul from them and destroy it with fiery wrath.

Their eyes fall to Zane. My Zane, whose chest doesn't move with the cadence of life. His stillness and ashen complexion announce his death as loud as my Book of Fates had.

I want to crawl to him, to touch him, to breathe air back in his lungs, but he remains still, with that damned scythe laying across his chest.

Zane sacrificed his life for me.

Tears blur my vision, and I close the distance, but resist reaching out. I cover my face, ignoring the whoosh of the sliding glass doors. It isn't until a hand touches my shoulder that I look up into my father's eyes. He crouches next to me and wipes a stray tear off my cheek.

"I need to go," he says softly and gives me a sad smile.

"Why?" I blink, not understanding why he'd abandon me when I need him the most.

191

"It's part of the deal. You should know that better than anyone." He glances at Zane to make his point.

But I don't know. He hadn't died when I took the role, so why now?

If he had known, I would bet my life that Zane never would have done this. He would have never sacrificed himself knowing someone else would die instead, especially my father—because without a soul, this was the end for him.

He will turn to ashes the moment his life is snuffed out.

My chest squeezes. "Don't go, Daddy," I sob. "Please," I whisper. I can't have both of them out of reach, one permanently, the other figuratively. "You don't have a soul. If you go with them, you'll cease to exist, just like that reaper."

He takes my hands between his and squeezes gently. "Have a little faith. Besides, I need to teach Zane a few things before he comes back." My father hooks his thumb toward my dead boyfriend. "Things you safeguarded us from. Otherwise, he will be more of a menace to the living than you can imagine. Your touch may strip souls, but his will kill."

My heart lurches in my chest. "But..." I glance at Zane.

"His touch kills the living, and that includes you, Melissa." He slowly stands. "So, let me go train him in Purgatory and try to release our old friend while I'm at it. Just don't move him, okay? You can throw a blanket over him if that makes you feel better, but do not let anyone touch him."

I nod. I don't want Zane gone into the reaper realm forever. I need him for so many reasons. He promised to help me sort out this abysmal touch curse, to make it disappear.

"I love you, Missy. Promise me you won't do anything stupid, no matter what happens," my father says.

I nod, thinking he's talking about Zane. "I promise." Tears spill, creating hot paths down my cheeks.

He smiles and then he turns and heads toward the angel horde in a gait that's more arrogant than humbled. When he spreads his arms wide, it's not in a manner of surrender; it is pure mockery.

"No!" A muffled voice comes from inside the house, yanking my attention that way. My mother struggles to break free of Alex's grasp. She looks like a wild woman trying to scratch her way out as she screams.

When I look back, I catch the sharp edge of a golden sword sticking out of my father's back.

Now I know why my mother is going ape shit. I climb to my feet as well, bellowing the same "No!" as my mother.

I want to rush them, slaughter them for killing my father. The only thing that keeps me in place besides the angels' warning glares is my father's last words. If I attack, he'd perceive that as a stupid move, and I promised him I wouldn't do anything stupid.

Without the power of Death in my veins alongside Fate's energy, I cannot win a war waged with the angels. But that doesn't stop the devastation from filling me. How is my father supposed to train Zane when he's dead?

The blade disappears, pulled from his limp body, and I expect him to turn to ash like the reaper. But he doesn't. He just crumples to the ground. My mind snaps to the orbs circling us when Death's essence transitioned into Zane.

Could that have released the souls trapped inside me? And following on the heels of that thought: *Does this mean I'm no longer cursed?*

My mother collapses inside the house. She sobs his name over and over, and my heart breaks for her. The angels gather my father up, and in a whirlwind of smoke and light, they all disappear, but not before one of them points at me as if they aren't done with me yet.

A part of me wants to throw myself over Zane's body. If I die, so be it. At least I won't have to see the horrified sorrow on my mother's face every day of her life. But that's another stupid move, and neither my father nor Zane would be happy with me. Zane probably would be more pissed than he already was.

I need something to cling to now that the only human being I really care to hug is gone, and I have no idea if he'll make it back to me or not. So, I resolve to fix this damn curse, so when he comes back to me, I can kiss him into oblivion.

Besides, although Zane's actions seemed to defuse the angels' wrath, I don't know if any of us are truly safe from Heaven's retribution.

The End

Continue reading THE DEATH CHRONICLES II with REAP THE DEAD.

196

ABOUT J.E. TAYLOR

J.E. Taylor is a USA Today bestselling author, a publisher, an editor, a manuscript formatter, a mother, a wife, a business analyst, and a Supernatural fangirl. Not necessarily in that order. She first sat down to seriously write in February of 2007 after her daughter asked:

"Mom, if you could do anything, what would you do?"
From that moment on, she hasn't looked back.

Besides being co-owner of Novel Concept Publishing, Ms. Taylor also moonlights as a Senior Editor of Allegory E-zine, an online venue for Science Fiction, Fantasy and Horror, and co-host of the popular YouTube talk show Spilling Ink.

She lives in New Hampshire with her husband and during the summer months enjoys her weekends on the shore in southern Maine.

Visit her at www.jetaylor75.com to check out her other titles and sign up for her newsletter for early previews of her upcoming books, release announcements, and special opportunities for free swag!

198

If you liked FINDING DEATH, you should check out the rest of the books in THE DEATH CHRONICLES II:

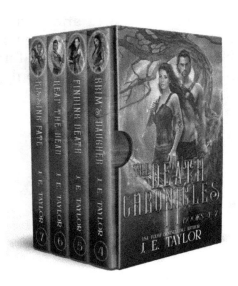

THE DEATH CHRONICLES II

Death is the family business, but not one I want to pursue. Thankfully, it's been passed down from father to son for generations, so it should skip me as Death's daughter. Then I won't have to stop being alive and can actually live my life. Right?

Well, the reapers don't agree. And neither do the angels.

One thinks I'm destined to take over, the other believes I will destroy existence. Both want me dead to match their own agendas.

I have an agenda of my own, and Leviathan who has sworn to protect me. But once my family and friends start being targeted, the family business, while grim, might be the only choice I have to save those I love.

The Death Chronicles *II* includes the following titles

Grim's Daughter

Finding Death

Reap the Dead

Kissing Fate

You might also like these other titles set in the same world as THE DEATH CHRONICLES II:

THE RYAN CHRONICLES

Demons, vampires, angels, and the devil. What the hell kind of nightmare do I live in?

CJ Ryan was born with enough psychic power to destroy the earth. And Lucifer wants him to do just that.

Raised with a strong moral compass, CJ won't sacrifice innocent lives to protect his own, and that puts him at odds with the devil.

But if he doesn't give in, he and all he loves will become the target of Lucifer's rage.

When CJ gives his twin brother, Tom, a dose of
his powers to keep him safe, it puts Tom directly
in Lucifer's crosshairs.

As the final battle draws near, what will they
have to sacrifice to keep their loved ones safe?

Can they survive the devil's wrath?

THE RYAN CHRONICLES includes these titles:

CJ's Story:

ANGEL GRACE - Book 1

ANGEL HEART - Book 2

ANGEL WRATH – Book 3

Tom's Story:

ANGEL BLOOD - Book 4

ANGEL FIRE - Book 5

ANGEL FURY – Book 6

Fans of Supernatural and Shadowhunters will
enjoy this series.

FIRE CURSED TRILOGY

Lucifer's daughter rises.

Faith Kennedy's mother hid the awful truth from her daughter for sixteen years. Until she lay on her deathbed. Only then did she reveal who sired her daughter, and the revelation terrifies Faith.

The devil may have sired her, but he only wants her beating heart ripped out of her chest. After all, that's where her angel grace fueling her fire power is stored, and that will give him what he needs to bring about humanity's fall.

And Lucifer will take down anyone who gets in his way.

When Faith is given an ancient knife that can kill the devil, she faces the toughest challenge of her young life. She must hunt Lucifer and put him down. Otherwise, the world will burn.

But if she succeeds, she may wipe herself, and everyone she loves, out of existence.

This set includes Fire Cursed, Homecoming, and Judgement Day.

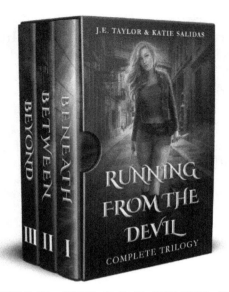

RUNNING FROM THE DEVIL TRILOGY

An escaped demon and a snarky cat face off against the seven deadly sins.

Escaping from Hell was just the beginning of Phoebe's problems. In Hell, she had a position of legend. A marquis of torture. But on the human plane, she is just another New York City destitute.

Before she has a chance to get her bearings on the unforgiving streets, Fate steps in and offers her a chance at redemption, but it doesn't come cheap.

She must bring in the demons that escaped alongside her while making sure no humans are harmed in the process. In order to do that, she needs to learn to live in the human world with the help of another one of Fate's parolees, a snarky cat named Smoke.

If it means never seeing the halls of Hell again, Phoebe will do anything, even battle the seven deadly sins single-handed.

Find these titles and other fantasy and suspense titles on J.E. Taylor's website!

www.JETaylor75.com

Printed in the USA
CPSIA information can be obtained
at www.ICGtesting.com
LVHW041304070624
782576LV00007B/729